Praise For

"The Major & The Musician"

"Fueled by love, laced with mystery—this work doesn't whisper, it roars."

-Major Jennifer Bradley, USAF, Retired

"When it comes to the advice, it comes across as knowing and seasoned, yet compassionate and filled with love. It is like a big sister who wants to take the pain from the journey while allowing for the individual's growth."

- Lisa Lively

"The Major and The Musician champions all moms! You are seen, heard, and valued."

- Brandy Grillo

The Major & The Musician
A Warrior Mom Mystery

Bren Harris

SayThat Publishing

Contents

Introduction

TWO YEARS AGO
2359 Hours (Almost midnight)
New Year's Eve - Washington, D.C.

"5 - 4 - 3 - 2 - 1, HAPPY NEW YEAR!" The chant fills the grand ballroom of the Washington, D.C., Waldorf Astoria as confetti showers down, glinting against the chandeliers. Crystal champagne flutes clink in celebratory toasts. As my spotlight dims to a gentle glow, the band transitions into a soft melody, welcoming the new year. The air is thick with the crisp scent of champagne and the rich perfume of elegantly dressed guests. I glide offstage left, my hand-beaded jumpsuit catching the light with every step.

The Waldorf Astoria crowd is always a solid New Year's Eve gig for us. Rushing backstage, I aim for a quick New Year's Eve kiss, a perfect moment for my social media, with my fiancé before our next music set.

"Jameson! Where are you?" I whisper-shout in the dimly lit hallway. *How did I ever fall for a Washington lobbyist? That cheating jerk! After the holidays, I'm so done with him.*

A sharp crash intensifies my steps. Heart pounding, I push through the door to the green room and freeze. Jameson lies on the floor, a dark pool of blood spreading around his head. I stifle a scream, turning to flee the sudden nightmare. Panic constricts my chest; my thoughts scatter in terror as tears blur my vision.

A glowing red exit sign beckons me to a side door. I blindly rush down the stairs to a service exit, desperate for air. Outside, I gulp in the cool winter breeze, craving oxygen. Snowflakes gently fall, melting on my sparkling sleeve. The stench of vomit hits me, and I realize I'm the one dry-heaving in the alley. Cold sweat clings to my damp skin. I shiver as gloved hands suddenly grab me from behind, choking the air out of me.

"Keep your mouth shut or you'll be next, Princess," he growls, then throws me to the ground. His heavy footsteps echo as he rushes toward 11th Street.

Run! Get up and run right now! Scrambling, I sprint, not thinking it through, and run in the opposite direction, straight into a brick wall of masculine heat and strength.

"Let go of me! I promise I won't say anything. Just let me go!" I plead with forced bravado.

"Ash, it's me," a familiar baritone voice soothes. "You're safe. Come on, let's get you warm." Just like that, Major Anthony Ransom II, the son of Vice President Anthony Ransom Sr., carefully helps me into a black Suburban driven by his security detail.

"Deuce?" because he hates being called Junior "What are you doing here?"

"I came to see you play your New Year's Eve gig, silly girl. Why else?" he replies with a slight Texas drawl.

Huh? Why is my college sweetheart swooping in like a modern-day Marvel hero?

"Dad keeps me posted when I'm deployed. I just scheduled my leave so I could be in town."

We coast effortlessly down Pennsylvania Avenue, past the White House, onto Dupont Circle.

"My fiancé... He's dead," I hiccup with a sob. "I just bolted!"

"Did that thug in the alley have something to do with it?"

WHAM! A navy blue Hummer t-bones us. I can't see.

"Ash, wake up. We gotta get out of here. NOW!" Deuce whispers urgently. "Can you move? Can you run? Are you hurt?"

My head pounds like the worst hangover. "Did you say fun? No, I am NOT having fun. My ears are ringing!" I shout.

"Yep, you must've hit your head. I said RUN. Let's move."

We squeeze through the sunroof one at a time. Blood trickles into my right eye. Deuce doesn't look much better.

"What happened?"

"We'll catch up later. Let's get back to the hotel. I have a suite there under an alias for tonight. We'll be safe there for now."

"An alias? Wait, what's going on?"

In honor of the late Grandpa Harris, pictured here serving on the island of Okinawa (1945-1946).

Thank you to all who serve.

South Island

Where Naha and Shuri Castle and are located

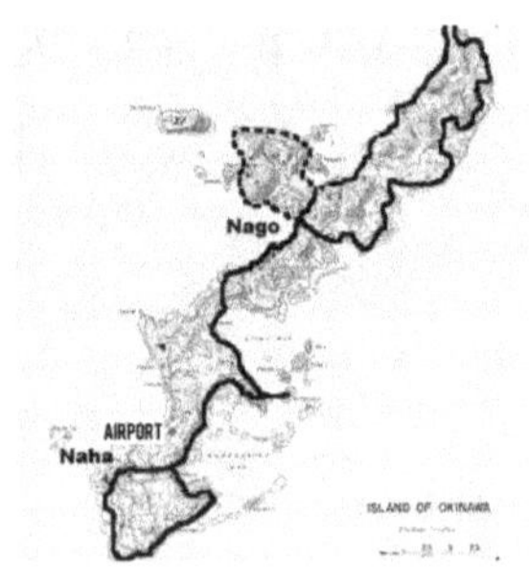

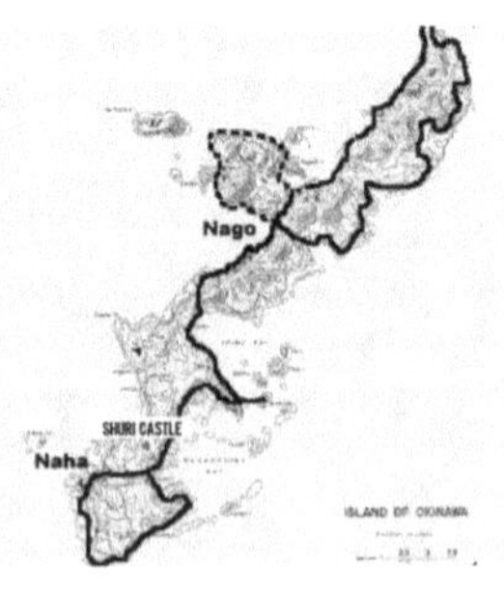

Chapter One

The Torii Gate

Boundary - Protection - Welcoming - Respect

PRESENT DAY - 2 Years Later

Friday, 1500 Hours (3pm)

Airport - Naha, Okinawa (South Island)

My heart races with adrenaline when the van door slams shut with a punishing *ssshhhwack!* The stifling weather on Okinawa, this tiny Japanese island, just over a thousand miles south of Tokyo, is suffocating in its heat and humidity.

Just then, a group of locals swiftly shuffles past. Thirty tour group members, each about 4' 10", are uniformly dressed in polyester taupe slacks and Kariyushi shirts, their vibrant take on the Hawaiian shirt.

"These tour groups... What is it with the wardrobe strategy?" I mutter to myself, a hint of impatience in my tone.

My mother, affectionately known as Gigi to her grandchildren, blends in seamlessly, standing at a proud 5' tall with her salt-and-pepper pixie cut. Having her here has been a blessing, especially with the new baby.

I tap her on the arm. "Hey, make sure you have your passport. Oh! And keep your phone charged. I want to reach you during your layover in Tokyo."

She rolls her eyes with a finesse that outdoes my teenage rebellious phase. "For the third time, I've got it. Let's focus on this handsome grandson of mine."

I shove the stroller towards the elevators while slinging the diaper bag over my shoulder like a roadie at a rock concert, hoping we make it to the airline counter on time.

Four months have flown by. My mother, who's never traveled outside the States, is ready to return to Texas. I, however, wish she would stay here in southern Japan until my husband's military assignment is over and done–with a capital D.

Then it hits me: we've been married for nearly two years. How is that even possible? The Major and I rekindled our love, married, and moved overseas in a whirlwind of 90 days. That crazy scene at the Waldorf Astoria really was one for the record books. We still didn't know who killed my former fiancé...I use the term fiancé loosely when referring to Jameson. He was such a cheat!

Back to happier thoughts, I hear my grandmother say, "When you know, you know," and she was right.

I sigh and whisper to myself, "Major and Mrs. Anthony Ransom, II. Yep, Nanny, you were absolutely right."

I'll never forget the unchecked pride on Nanny's face when I sang at my wedding. When she realized my dashing husband was accompanying me on his 12-string acoustic Martin, I thought her sprightly eighty-year-young self might dance on the tables.

"Hello? Earth to Ashley!" Gigi interrupts, waving her hand in front of my face.

"Sorry, just reliving my amazing wedding... again," I reply sheepishly.

"I get it. But right now, I need some direction instead of your trip down memory lane," she teases, nudging me with her elbow and giving me a knowing wink.

We hurry to the counter, just making it in time. Behind us, caterers in crisp white uniforms haul a massive silver tray loaded with an exotic array of fish heads adorned with caviar and garlic.

"Why do they always dress alike?" Gigi asks, her curiosity piqued.

"It's cultural, more of a local thing. Mainland Japan doesn't seem to do that, " I explain.

We finally collapse into a quiet corner of the airport, a rarity here, sinking into the luxurious comfort of low-slung, handmade chairs. Gigi gently lifts baby Liam from the stroller and cradles him close. It's a heartwarming scene, and I hate to see her go.

Tears well up in my eyes as I choke them back, realizing just how much I'll miss having my mom around.

WHOMP!

Suddenly, a teen in a red hoodie slams into our stroller as he tries to hurdle it. His toe catches on the top handle, sending it spinning across the lobby.

"Hey, idiot! Watch it!" The words escape my lips before I can censor my frustration. Liam starts wailing as the perpetrator rights the stroller and disappears into a side door of the concourse.

"Oh, honey, he was probably just late for his flight. It'll all work out," Gigi murmurs, soothing Liam back to sleep.

"Well, he's an idiot. He could've at least apologized." I grunt. *Whoa, this sleep deprivation is dangerous*, I think to myself.

I inspect the stroller for damage while Gigi sings softly to Liam.

"Who are you and what have you done with my mother?!" I joke, using humor to deflect the heaviness of the moment.

The tangy scent of curry clings to my waist-length hair. The stroller feels heavier than usual, but I chalk it up to exhaustion. "I need coffee. No, scratch that, might as well chew on this phone charger, I'm so tired."

"All new moms feel that way. Don't worry. Just sleep when Liam does, and you'll feel back to normal soon," Gigi advises sagely.

"Thanks, Mom. Listen, we call them hurricanes in Texas, but here in Japan, they're called typhoons. We really need to get you on that plane before this storm hits."

Feeling like a mopey fifth grader at my first school dance, I awk-wardly walk her to the security scanners. A piece of my heart is leaving today. Overwhelmed with grief, Liam and I watch until Gigi success-fully navigates through security.

We slowly make our way back to our little Scooby van on the third floor of the parking garage. Seriously, the thing looks like a small loaf of bread, it cracks me up every time I drive it.

After clicking the rear-facing car seat into place, I rush to the left driver's seat, only to find no steering wheel. Exhausted, I remember and shuffle to the right-side front seat, Japan's driving norms still catching me off guard. Feels very British to drive on the right side.

As we head north on Highway 58 toward the base, Shuri Castle looms in imperial red, its rumored secret tunnels linked to the Yakuza, a stark contrast to the island's low crime rate. Local laws allow authorities to hold suspects without evidence for up to 52 days, a concept I find unnerving.

A motorcycle cuts sharply in front of us, its rider attempting a risky maneuver. I swerve, hitting the only pothole in sight with a jarring thud. The rider crashes into a lamp post. "Stupid human tricks for $500, Alex," I mumble, unapologetically.

Liam's cries from the backseat fray my already tense nerves. Pulling into the 100 Yen Store parking lot, I double park amidst the pre-storm rush.

Hopping out, I round the van quickly to tend to Liam. A foul odor assaults my senses. "Now you decide to poop...when Gigi leaves and your daddy is deployed off the island!" I mutter. Realizing I'm now truly alone as a new mom, panic flutters in my chest. *Deep breaths. You got this.*

As I change Liam, a local driver honks impatiently. I signal 'another minute, please, arigato', humming "Mr. Roboto" to lighten the mood. *Relax, mister. At least I remembered the word for thank you in Japanese, right?*

Immediately, I realize that might not have been my smartest move. The delivery driver is now storming toward us, hurling Japanese expletives. Shaking, I quickly secure the still-crying Liam back into his carrier and hop into the driver's seat.

I sing, I coo, I beg, I plead. Nothing quiets Liam until we approach the Torii Gate. His eyes fixate on the bright red, pi-shaped structure, instantly mesmerized. I can almost hear my favorite math instructor, affectionately known as Boom Boom, reminding us, "3.14159, remember March 14th, we're celebrating Pi Day. Bring your favorite flavor!" A giggle escapes, as relief washes over me. The gate not only marks a boundary between the outside world and my sanctuary but also brings a welcome silence. "Why didn't I think of this earlier?" I mutter, handing Liam the bright red Torii Gate keychain my granddad gifted me when he passed away a few years ago.

We pull up to the base, winding through the serpentine entrance before queuing up at the gate. Liam contentedly gnaws on the keychain while a Security Forces member verifies my ID, and another guard motions us through.

I must admit, it feels a bit fancy, like living on a high-end gated ranch back in Texas.

Friday, 1600 Hours (4pm)
Major & Ashley Ransom's Home
Undisclosed Military Base - Okinawa

"Ahhh, home sweet *home-away-from-home*," I hum, unlatching the car seat from the back. We step inside our modest quarters, nothing extravagant, just a humble house with a million-dollar view.

I shift Liam into the soft, chest-hugging baby carrier and secure him gently against me. At four months old, he's still the perfect size for this. We head out to the lanai, and I immediately step in a fresh splatter of fruit bat guano.

"Ugh! No wonder they call you guys *flying foxes,* you drop your fruit bombs with strategic precision," I mutter, wiping it off with a trusty wet wipe. I refuse to let guano ruin the moment. The breeze is warm and slow, and the view, cobalt waves stretching across the East China Sea, wraps me in peace.

BEEP! BEEP! BEEP! The serenity vanishes as a high-pitched beeping slices through the air. Liam erupts in a wail, his little voice rising to match the alarm. I sway gently, trying to soothe him while my eyes scan the space.

Just as suddenly as it began, the sound stops. Silence returns like nothing happened.

"Well then. If it's important, it'll show itself," I murmur, shrugging off the unease.

I pour myself a small glass, two ounces, give or take, of *Lagrima Del Sol*, the local pineapple wine I've come to love. Settling into the filtered late afternoon light, I let the sweetness wash over me as I exhale into the moment.

Half an hour later, a rapid knock at the front door jolts me from my relaxation. I double-check that Liam is still soundly sleeping on me, grab my glass, and head to the door, appreciating the coolness of our concrete bunker-style home. Built in the 1950s, my HGTV-addict neighbor, Corinne, calls it mid-century modern...news to me.

Peering through the glass storm door, I see it's the Master Chief. "Hi there. Is everything okay?" I ask, a hint of concern in my voice.

"Pretty good, ma'am. Were you at the airport this afternoon? There's been an incident," he inquires.

"Yes, I dropped off my mom. She's headed back to the States."

"Well, the security footage shows that this young man bumped into you. Did you see him today?" He holds up his phone with a clear picture of the stroller-capsizing culprit.

"Yes! He knocked over the stroller we had with us. Really looked like he was in a hurry."

"OK then. I just thought I would check. I appreciate your cooperation," he says, his voice revealing a hint of tension. He pauses, then adds, "That young man is actually one of our newest recruits, and I'm trying to find him," almost growling the words.

"He was kind enough to help set the stroller back up after knocking it over," I quickly added, hoping to spare the recruit from severe consequences.

"Well, there's that, I guess. Thank you again for your time." He nervously fiddles with his hat, then runs his fingers through his dark hair. "And here, this belongs to Major Ransom." He hands me a sealed manila envelope and heads back to his vehicle.

Wondering what that was all about and why he seemed so anxious, I notice the envelope's addressed to Major and Mrs. Ransom. Curiosity piqued, I take a quick look inside:

In the place where lions refuse sleep,
a hidden path the duo seeks.
Find the gate where progress stands,
guarding secrets of monoreeru and man.
Find the flying fox's wings,
touch each tip concurrently.
Use the sacred keys aligned,
in the walls of the ancient shrine.
San de waru!

As the Torii Gate-shaped scar on my left hand begins to tingle, a sure sign of significance, I realize my brain simply doesn't have the energy to decipher this message right now. Opting for a simpler pleasure, I settle down to finish the final chapter of my latest fiction novel on the lanai. The soft breeze carries the scent of hope and brine, and the island's birds chirp musically, adding to the magic of this place.

An hour slips by, and concern for my mom nudges me back to reality. She's supposed to be on a long layover in Tokyo. I pick up my phone to check on her, only to be greeted by a frustrating busy signal. Again and again, the same tone, could she have forgotten to charge her phone? Despite her Sunday school teacher appearance, my mom is a fiercely protective mama bear. It seems I've inherited more than just her looks; her protective instincts are in me, too. I laugh softly. *Am I becoming a helicopter daughter? No, I'm just concerned, that's all.*

As I distractedly sort through a stack of papers heading out to the lanai, the persistent busy signals become a distant backdrop to my task. Suddenly, a vivid memory floods through me, overwhelming my senses. The wine glass slips from my grasp, shattering on the outdoor tiles, and as the shards scatter, so too does my consciousness. For a moment or two, I'm pulled back 27 years, to when I was just six years old, and my world fades to a distant, forgotten black.

27 Years Ago - September 1997
Texas Hill Country

Complete darkness envelops me, mingled with the stench of mold and decay, a scent reminiscent of my grandma's cellar, yet here I am, trapped in what feels like an abandoned well shaft. Goosebumps cover my bare arms as a spider tickles my right leg, prompting a shiver and a squeak to escape my lips.

My hands tingle painfully, as if fire ants are marching over them. Brushing hair from my face, I feel something sticky and wince, realizing there's a gash on my left hand. Panic sets in. Where's my granddad's keychain? I'm in deep trouble if I lost it when I fell. I shake my head, a bad idea, as more darkness clouds my vision. *I can't even remember my last name. Shouldn't a six-year-old be able to remember their last name?*

Distant voices pierce the silence. "HELP!" I try to scream, but it comes out only as a whimper. *Is this what Princess Diana felt like after her car accident? Cold, lonely, bleeding out, chased by bad guys,* images my mama replayed from the news. *Would she weep for me as she did for a princess far away?*

"Where did that brat go off to and hide?" I hear my mean teenage cousin Griffith's voice. "Her daddy carries a pistol everywhere. I ain't takin' the blame for your screw-up, boy!"

"How was I supposed to know she'd be faster than lightnin'?" another boy responds defensively.

I don't recognize his voice. Shouldn't I know the voice of someone told to watch me?

"You're an idiot. Why did I ever ask for your help?" Griffith's frustration boils over as he storms off. "She took Granddaddy's Torii Gate keychain. I was using it for target practice. I'm gonna find her and get it back, cuz it's gonna be mine. I'm the oldest cousin, that oughta mean somethin'," he spits venomously over his shoulder.

So that's what cut my hand! The pain is as fierce as a rabid dog bite. I try to call out again, but a chilling knowing silences me: I am not safe. No one is coming to save me. My small frame begins to tremble uncontrollably as I sink further into the inky blackness surrounding me.

PRESENT DAY
1800 Hours (6pm)
Major & Ashley Ransom's Home
Undisclosed Military Base - Okinawa

"WOOF!" The sudden sound startles me. Looking down, I find our one-year-old Labradoodle, Naki, pawing at my leg, begging for attention. The familiar tune of "Who Let the Dogs Out" starts playing in my head.

I grab a broom and methodically sweep up the broken glass from earlier, answering the song's rhetorical question with a weary smile. *Yes, it was me...I let the dog out. Well, just one dog, and she really needed a pit stop.* After ensuring the floor is safe, I lift Liam from his carrier. He snuggles against my chest, and I head inside and settle him into his crib, then collapse into the nearby rocker.

The memory that resurfaced was fleeting yet vivid, almost as if it happened for a reason. Will I ever be known as anything more than 'the girl who fell in the well'? What a media circus that was. I close my eyes, just for a moment, hoping for a brief escape.

The gentle patter of rain against the window evolves into a rhythmic tapping as Liam's cries suddenly pierce the calm. I spring from the rocker, touching his forehead...hot to the touch. Gently, I scoop him up, patting his back in a steady rhythm as I mentally prepare for what's next. The room is soon filled with the acrid smell of reflux, a benign word for a foul reality. His onesie, the sheets, and the handmade blanket from Gigi. All ruined.

"You couldn't give me 15 more minutes, kiddo?" I whisper as the room spins around me. If sleep deprivation were a torture technique, I'd have surrendered all my secrets long ago.

The ring of my phone cuts through the chaos. Balancing Liam on one hip, I hurry to the entry table. As I reach for the phone, a loud crash startles us both, the bedroom window shatters. Liam's scream intensifies. I whirl around to see a rock, wrapped in a piece of paper, resting in the chair we just left.

Trembling, I approach the rock, unwrap the paper, and read:

We know he gave it to you. We need it back. Or else.

The words send a shiver down my spine as I clutch Liam closer. My hands tremble as I manage to trap the phone between my shoulder and chin, barely muttering a shaky "hello."

"Hey there, Mrs. Ransom, it's Ms. Della with Command Central."

Lesson 1: Kugi Ichi

Moai [MO-aay] - I see you. You are safe here.

I SEE YOU, WARRIOR. Life might feel like a freight train barreling down the Autobahn right now.

One day, you're sipping wine on the beach, honeymooning in bliss. Today? You find yourself juggling 97 different responsibilities at once.

Add a special needs child to the mix? Well, much like a rock through a window, life shatters in an instant: CRASH!

Initially, shock sets in, leaving us numb. Then, the anger at such an injustice begins to consume us.

We might try to numb this overwhelming pain by any means necessary, just begging it to stop.

But I see you. I'm here for you. I'm holding space for you. Just observe.

When you encounter something you wish to change (to feel more comfortable), resist that initial impulse. Pause. Ask yourself: What is this trying to teach me right now? No need to respond. Just sit with it for the moment.

Remember, feelings aren't facts. They are just feelings. Allow yourself to truly feel them again, but with intention. Awareness is our practice for the next 24 hours.

Document each incident in **The Warrior Mom™ Journal**. You are capable of handling this, Warrior.

And always remember, I see you! Your Story Matters.

I am with you,

Bren

North Island

Where Pizza in the Sky and the General's compound are located

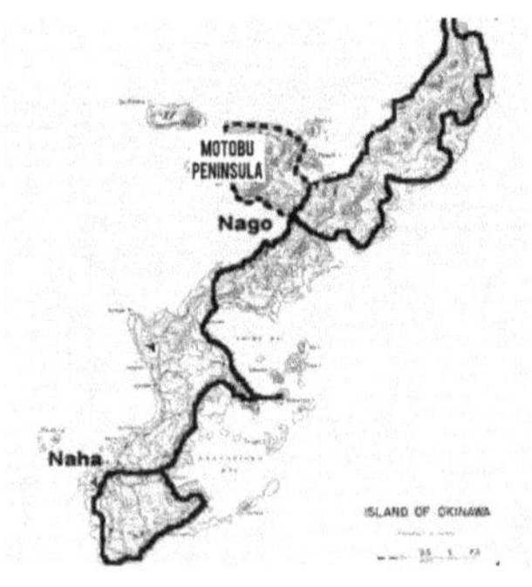

Chapter Two

Cho Ogata Taifu (Super Typhoon)

1900 Hours (7pm)
Major & Ashley Ransom's Home
Undisclosed Military Base - Okinawa

"Command Central?" I ask, my voice tinged with confusion.

"Yes, Ma'am," comes the reply from Della, the local godmother figure to all of us. Her voice is a mix of warmth and authority.

"I'm so glad you're calling. How did you know already?"

"Ashley, are you okay? How did we know what, exactly?"

"That someone just launched a rock, with a threatening note, through my son's bedroom window. There's glass everywhere!"

"Copy that. Are any of y'all hurt?"

"No, just a little freaked out."

"I'm dispatching our Security Forces Commander right now. Move to a safe part of the house and stay on the line with me, ya hear?"

"Okay. We're in the north end TV room. But wait, why were you calling me in the first place?"

"Oh, right. The Ghost Ops deployment team is delayed. Major Ransom won't be returning tomorrow as planned."

"Is it anything dangerous?" I ask, unable to mask the sharp edge of concern in my voice.

"The assignment has simply expanded. It's need-to-know, ya understand."

"Of course." I try to sound reassured, but the unease lingers. Suddenly, flashing lights cut through the dimming evening. "The Commander is here now."

"Excellent. You're in good hands. I hope you solve your mystery sooner rather than later. And give that precious baby a hug for me. Bye now."

***

"Mrs. Ransom, I'm Commander Heisler with Security Forces. We heard you had a little trouble. Can you point me in the right direction?" The Commander stands at the door, his raincoat soaked through as the storm winds begin to howl. Outside, I watch as my five-year-old neighbor's tricycle is hurled into the gnarled branches of the 200-year-old banyan tree in our front yard.

"Sure, come on in," I say, trying to keep my voice steady as I sway a screaming Liam in my arms, attempting to soothe him. "It's just through there on the left. We were resting after I took my mom to the airport. I got up to answer the phone because Command Central was calling. The moment I left that chair, a rock, wrapped in a note, came through the window. You can read it."

"Ah, it looks like someone's playing mind games here. We haven't had many incidents on base." Commander Heisler gestures to his crew, who start moving towards Liam's room. "I'll need to get my technicians in here to take pictures and dust for prints. In the meantime, can you walk me through what you think this might be about?" He pauses and adds, "Not to add to your stress, but you are prepared for this super typhoon, right?"

"Super typhoon?" I repeat, my voice catching.

"Copy. We'll have someone over to help once we clear the crime scene."

"Crime scene?" My voice rises slightly, betraying my growing anxiety.

"No worries. We'll get this place cleaned up too. It might take us a day or two. Do you have someone you could stay with to keep you and your son safe while Major Ransom is deployed?"

"Yes, I'll make a few calls while you guys do your CSI thing."

"Before you go, were either of you injured?"

"No. Both of us would've been if Command Central hadn't called."

"I understand and realize this is stressful. We'll get to the bottom of this," Commander Heisler assures me.

A loud knock at the door interrupts us. Commander Heisler motions for me to step back to safety behind the kitchen bar. I duck behind it, dialing my friend Corinne's number, as he strides to the door. His hand rests on the grip of his standard-issue Beretta M9 semi-automatic pistol.

***

As Corinne's voice fills my ear, I press the phone closer, my whisper barely audible over the howl of the storm outside.

"Corinne? It's Ashley. Hold on a sec. I'm in a situation," I say, my voice tense.

"Girl, what kind of situation, and why are you whispering?" Corinne's tone is a mix of concern and curiosity.

"The base's Security Forces team is here, and someone's at my door," I reply, keeping my voice low as I peek over the kitchen bar to see Commander Heisler approaching the door.

"Oooooh exciting!" Corinne's excitement is palpable even through the phone. "Why are they there, and who could possibly be at your door in this storm?"

"Just... hold on," I urge, my attention split as I watch the commander cautiously prepare to open the door. The wind picks up, sending a gust that shakes the windows, adding to the cacophony of the night.

From my vantage point, I can only see the back of Commander Heisler as he steps outside, his posture rigid, signaling caution. The tension in the room mounts, and I strain to hear any indication of what's happening at the front door.

***

The Commander positions himself defensively as he swings open the door, prepared for the worst. To his surprise, it's not an intruder but his close friend and colleague, Weapons Commander Jim Linus, who steps into the light.

"Hey, Jim. What are you doing here?" Commander Heisler asks, his confusion evident in his furrowed brow and the slight relaxation of his posture.

"Well, I heard there was some excitement over here. Thought I'd stop by and check it out for myself," Jim replies with a casual shrug, though his eyes scan the room with a trained vigilance.

The two men step inside, shutting the door against the howling wind. Commander Heisler's expression shifts from surprise to concern as he processes Jim's unexpected appearance.

"Excitement is one word for it," Heisler mutters, attempting to lead Jim away from the door and towards the heart of the house, where it's safer. "We've got a rock through the window, a threatening note, and now a super typhoon on the way. Not exactly the quiet evening we all had planned."

Jim nods, his demeanor serious. "I heard about the typhoon, but a threatening note? Sounds like you've got a real situation on your hands."

***

"Psst... Corinne, it's just Commander Linus," I whisper into the phone, my voice barely above a breath.

"Wait, Jim Linus? Well, their wives are thick as thieves, you know," Corinne quickly divulges, her tone dropping to a conspiratorial murmur. "If they could, those two would ditch their husbands and start a commune for mean girls. They both call him 'Spineless Linus' behind his back. I swear, Barbie and Lacey need to grow up!" I can almost hear the eye roll through the phone, her gossip addiction taking precedence even in less-than-ideal times.

"Really? I'm still new around here. Good to know, I guess," I respond, a bit overwhelmed but grateful for the intel. "Hey, Liam and

I might need a place to crash while the team cleans up our house. Someone threw a rock through one of our bedroom windows."

"They did what?!" Corinne's voice spikes with shock and concern.

"Long story. We're fine, just a bit rattled. I'll fill you in later." I glance over my shoulder, still unsure why I'm whispering while crouched behind the kitchen bar.

"Can't wait to hear all about it. I'll have the guest room ready for you," she assures me, her voice brimming with anticipation for the details. "I want the full scoop, my friend. Leave no stone unturned!"

***

Commander Linus lingers by the front door, watching the scene unfold with an uneasy stance. Commander Heisler speaks to him in a low, stern tone.

"Well, this really isn't your area, Jim. Aren't you on the night shift for weapons duty? I heard it was a punishment-detail for failing your Physical Fitness test."

"Yeah, I know, but it was just so dull there. And come on, we're practically brothers. Our wives are inseparable. I just thought I might lend a hand," Linus replies, his voice tinged with a mix of defensiveness and eagerness.

"No, you need to head back to the munitions dump. This is an active crime scene, and I can't have non-essential personnel involved," Heisler asserts firmly, leaving no room for argument.

As Linus opens his mouth to respond, a sudden, deafening **KA-BOOM!** shatters the tension. An explosion rocks the neighborhood, sending a shockwave through the house. Concrete dust billows into the room, clouding the air and coating everything in a fine grey powder.

Stunned, Linus drops his phone and stares blankly towards the source of the blast.

Coughing and shielding Liam with my body, I leap to my feet. With the house still trembling from the aftershock, I clutch Liam tightly and dart out the front door, desperate to escape any potential follow-up explosions or structural collapses.

Outside, the air is thick with confusion, and the echo of the explosion still rings in the air. I look back just in time to see Linus and Heisler, following quickly, their expressions a mix of shock and urgency.

"Stay with me, Liam," I whisper, sprinting towards what I hope will be safety, away from the chaos erupting behind us. The commanders are right on our heels, calling out commands to each other over the din of alarmed shouts and the howling wind.

1915 hours (7:15pm)
"Pizza In The Sky" Restaurant
Motobu Peninsula, Okinawa (North Island)
Barbie Heisler maneuvers the car into a parking spot on the cliff next to the iconic "Kajinho! Pizza In The Sky," her favorite spot for clandestine meet-ups. "I'm glad we aren't here with those loser witches," she mutters as she grips the steering wheel tightly.

"Hey, make sure your phone's turned off. We don't need anyone tracking where we are right now," Barbie reminds sharply as she kills the engine.

Lacey sighs, fumbling with her phone before switching it off. "I can't believe my 'Spineless Linus' didn't pass his freaking Physical

Training test. He's at risk of losing his command. How am I supposed to manage his career from the sidelines?"

"Oh, girl, we'll sort it out. Maybe even if we have to sneak him so me... help," Barbie suggests with a mischievous wink, trying to lighten the mood.

Lacey's eyes widen. "I could never...what about random drug tests?"

"Don't worry about that. My husband's a commander, too. I'll get the heads up on drug test schedules and let you know. You've got nothing to worry about," Barbie assures her with a conspiratorial grin.

They select their favorite table with a view, just as a server approaches with a flight of local sake. Lacey downs her first shot hastily, coughing a bit on the final sip. "You know, I've been steering Jim's career for the last decade, and he still hasn't made Colonel. Something's got to give. I need to up my game."

***

"I love you, Okasan. This is Soba, he's my new puppy. I found him, so now I get to keep him," declares five-year-old Kazuriyi, his eyes gleaming with the thrill of his new friendship.

"Of course, my precious son. Anything you want, you make it yours. Always remember, you are royalty and no one says no to royalty, understood?" confirms Cherry Blossom, her voice soft yet edged with the steel of her lineage as a fourth-generation Yakuza female assassin.

"Yes, Okasan." Kaz nods, his innocence shadowed by the weight of his heritage. "Come here, Soba, before the staff turns you into soba soup." His giggle fills the hallway as he scoops up the puppy. The two of them, fluffy and exuberant, bound up the stairs, embodying pure joy.

Cherry Blossom watches them go, her face a mask of maternal affection that slips for a moment to reveal the calculating coldness required of her profession. "Now, you two go play in your room while I get the staff to handle dinner," she calls after them, turning towards the kitchen to relay her orders.

As the sound of paws and little feet fades, she pauses, reflecting on the dual life she leads and the world her son must navigate, a world where loyalty, power, and danger intertwine daily.

***

Oyaban, the newly appointed Yakuza General on Okinawa, strides into the Tebori Tattoo studio nestled at the back of his sprawling estate on the Motobu Peninsula. A green smoky haze of handcrafted sumi ink engulfs the space, carrying with it the sharp scent of freshly burnt oil, a signature of Yokohama Tebori Tattoo Master, Horiyoshi III. The decision to fly him in from mainland Japan was nothing short of brilliant.

Horiyoshi III, renowned for his unparalleled skill, is here to create a masterpiece, a dragon emblazoned in Dragon's Breath Red-1A, a custom blend of ink. His tools are traditional; no machinery like the Americans use, everything is exquisitely crafted by hand.

The General is scheduled for a session each afternoon throughout the week, enduring the painstaking process with a large, slanted tool, without any painkillers. It is a rite of passage, a mark of his status as a Yakuza General. This dragon will be the crowning jewel of his Irezumi, his full-body tattoo, or "suit," as some refer to it in hushed tones.

In Japan, where tattoos are still far from mainstream, members of the Yakuza must be strategic about their ink. Even a Yakuza General can lounge poolside, his shirt open, sleeves rolled up just once, and never reveal his $100K full-body artwork to the uninitiated. Only the finest for Yakuza royalty.

As the session progresses, the General bites down on a leather strap, his face stoic, betraying no sign of pain. Tap, tap, punch. Wipe the excess ink. Tap, tap, punch. Wipe the excess ink. The rhythm of the tattooing seems to sync with the pelts of rain against the studio windows, each drop echoing the methodical puncture of skin.

This sequence is repeated thousands of times in one session. To the General, pain is merely weakness leaving the body, a weakness he refuses to acknowledge. With each penetration of the slanted hand tool, he mentally recites the names of his enemies, plotting their downfall. Exiled by mainland Yakuza, they see his displacement as a break in his power. They are gravely mistaken. This island, under his rule, thrives, and his reign of silent warfare has only just begun. He will show them that even in forced solitude, he is a force to be reckoned with.

1955 hours (7:55pm) -
"Kajinho/Pizza in The Sky" Restaurant,
Motobu Peninsula, Okinawa (North Island)

"Let's order another round of sake while we strategize. I mean, just look at this place...it's heaven. Despite the rain, we've got a terrific view of the East China Sea, the island of Ie Shima, and great pizza and local sake right here at Pizza In The Sky. What could possibly go wrong?" Barbie says, gesturing expansively at the panoramic scene framed by sheets of rain.

"You're not recording this conversation, are you?!" Lacey half-jokes, half-worries, her eyes scanning around as if expecting hidden mics, her nervous laughter barely masking her anxiety.

"Of course not! I save that trick for the witches, just in case I need some leverage." Barbie chuckles, her tone dripping with disdain for their absent frenemies. "And don't worry, we'll sort everything out. Spineless will have his command back within a week," she asserts with a confidence that seems both rehearsed and genuine.

Lacey nods, her expression a mix of relief and skepticism, as she raises her glass for another pour. "Well, here's to 'sorting things out' then," she says, the flickering candle on their table casting shadows that dance like the doubts in her mind.

As the server arrives with a fresh bottle of sake, the clink of the ceramic cups sounds almost ominous against the backdrop of the stormy sea, the laughter of the two women tinged with an edge of desperation. Their casual demeanor does little to mask the high stakes of their clandestine meeting, each sip of sake fortifying them for the manipulations ahead.

***

Sweat beads on The General's forehead, tracing a path down his left temple as waves of pain radiate down his spine and sear through his right leg. *Focus. Breathe. This is a rite of passage for leadership*, he coaches himself, steeling his resolve against the agony.

"General, the package you are expecting just arrived," comes the hushed, respectful murmur of one of his lieutenants from the doorway. The man bows deeply, embodying the deference owed to his rank and pain.

"Take it to my study. I will join you shortly. Dismissed," The General commands without turning, his voice firm despite the distraction of pain.

As the lieutenant's footsteps retreat, The General allows himself a moment to anticipate what comes next. This package is the keystone of the plan he has been meticulously crafting since his banishment to this remote island. *Now, the next phase of my plan is ready*, he thinks, a grim smile flickering across his face. He rises slowly, mastering his discomfort, driven by the promise of retribution and infinite power.

***

As the rain intensifies, winds whip fiercely, obscuring the view of Ie Shima Island from the balcony. "We'd better start heading back to base soon. I don't like this weather at all," Lacey murmurs, her voice barely audible over the howling storm as she finishes off their third round of sake.

Barbie nods, hastily grabbing her keys. She slips off her Jimmy Choos and sprints across the gravel parking area, feeling the rain pelting her face.

The two women dive into the car, and Barbie races away from the cliffside restaurant. She clenches the steering wheel tightly with one hand and fumbles to turn on her phone with the other as she rounds a curve on the Motobu Peninsula.

Just as the car takes the corner, five-year-old Kaz scoops up his puppy, Soba, from the middle of the dark road. Barbie swerves sharply, the car's side mirror clips the boy's right arm, sending both Kaz and his new puppy, Soba, tumbling. The car spins wildly, reminiscent of a stunt from a Fast and Furious movie. Kaz's scream cuts through the storm.

From the nearby mansion, the only one along this stretch of island road, a nanny rushes out. She scoops up Kaz and Soba, whispering reassuring words as she hurries them into the safety of their whitewashed mansion perched on the cliff overlooking the East China Sea.

Back in his study, The General is startled by the commotion.

"What is going on?" he demands. The nanny sets down Kaz and the puppy, her hands tremble from the crashing adrenaline as it turns to fear under The General's imposing gaze.

"The puppy ran into the street, and Kaz went after him. Some reckless driver was speeding and hit him. I'm so sorry, General, I should have been more vigilant," the nanny stammers, bowing deeply in both reverence and apology.

"WHO DARES HARM MY ONLY HEIR?" The General's voice booms with fury.

Kaz, still shaken, points towards the window. "Americans, on the side of the road."

Without hesitation, The General calls his Kobuns (lieutenants). They rush out to investigate and find Barbie and Lacey unconscious in their car, teetering precariously on the edge of the cliff.

Lesson 2: Kugi Nu

Atto Suru – Overwhelm

I SEE YOU, MOM!

There are days when you feel like you're juggling twenty plates at once, just like Ashley, dealing with a crying baby, a rock through her window, a commander at her door, and a typhoon raging outside. It seems like you're doing everything for everyone, and yet, it feels like no one notices. But I see you. I see each of you, Mamas. Let me be one hundred percent real with you right now: sometimes, life just *lifes*. And despite the endless list of tasks we complete, there's always that comment at the end of the day, like: "You know what this dinner needs to make it taste even better?" And YES! That's exactly when I imagine going full Scarlett Johansson as "Black Widow" on them... in my mind at least.

This Week: Take Five for Yourself. Please set aside just five minutes each day this week to write your very own "I see you, Mom" letter to yourself. Focus on acknowledging the unseen labor and emotional work you do daily. Write it out in **The Warrior Mom™ Journal.**

Read Your Letter Aloud: We, as moms, often feel unnoticed, yet we accomplish incredible things every day. It doesn't matter if the tasks are big or small; take a moment to embrace and compliment yourself for just doing them.

Encourage Self-Compassion: Recognizing your own efforts is essential for maintaining emotional well-being. Your mental and emotional health are crucial. **Remember, a rising tide lifts all boats**. When we acknowledge and elevate ourselves, we uplift those we love the most.

Create Community: Indeed, community is our secret weapon. Hard work is essential, but support from others can make all the difference. <u>Join our online Tribe*</u> to share stories and affirmations that make this motherhood journey a community effort. I would be honored to read your own "I see you, Mom!" letter there when you're ready.

Together, we are stronger.

I am with you,

Bren

Chapter Three

The Kintsugi Principle

2100 HOURS (9PM)

Corinne's House

Undisclosed Military Base - Okinawa

"Hey, TK. Tay and Baby Bear are secure at the HGTV Smart Bunker for a few days. Long story. It's all good. Hope this storm isn't giving you too much trouble. Please know we're thinking of you," I hesitantly leave the voicemail, hoping the coded message conveys enough without saying too much.

"Ashley Lynn Ransom! What in the world was that cryptic message?" Corinne chides with a giggle as she prepares her signature herbal tea for us.

"It's a coded system we thought up whenever he's on a mission. You know how it is with these Ghost Ops guys, always thinking nine steps ahead. Nothing too personal, all very need-to-know. For now, we can't go wrong referencing the Chiefs' Tight End and Time's Person of the Year," I explain, winking at her as I break into my best impression of a dance move from our favorite era, then quickly turning to feed Naki her evening kibbles.

"Well, I think it's adorable. You two are such newlyweds. I swear," Corinne teases, handing me a warm cup of tea.

"Ugh! I'm missing him and his bear hugs right now. When did I get this romantic?" I sigh, feeling the absence of my husband more acutely amidst the chaos of recent events.

"Don't ever worry about that. Hey, let's recap everything we know so far. Hopefully, we can get some answers before he gets home. Then you two can escape up north and start working on Liam's baby sister or brother," Corinne suggests with a mischievous eyebrow wiggle.

"Slow your roll, girl. I'm barely functioning with one child right now!" I laugh, shaking my head at her enthusiasm for expanding *my* family.

"Hey, how's your gig as the personal chef for the wing commander?" I ask, steering the conversation towards her life, eager to shift away from my own tumultuous thoughts.

Corinne sets down her tea, her face lighting up with the kind of excitement that only comes from doing something you love. "It's amazing! I mean, it's a challenge, but I get to be creative every day. And you wouldn't believe the kind of stories these pilots have!"

She pours another round of tea, the steam carrying away some of the tension in the room.

"The Wing Commander is fantastic. But the local wealthy business wives? They're a whole other story. We're entertaining them all next week, and the menu planning feels like strategizing in the final two minutes of the Super Bowl with the ball on the one-yard line!" Corinne clears her throat and adopts a haughty accent, "We are NOT using frozen mint. We are NOT using dried mint. It must be fresh mint for the mojitos, and they must be skinny mojitos." As she mimics their demands, wind and rain lash against the window beside us, punctuating her performance.

"Because apparently, everyone needs to watch their waistline," she rolls her eyes and sighs, the sarcasm dripping from her words.

"Girl, you are so good for me," I laugh-cry, genuinely amused. "You should really consider stand-up with all this material you have." I pull out a bottle of pumped breast milk from her fridge. "I'll feed Liam while we sit and catch up on everything."

Corinne follows us into her living room, her fancy tray of herbal tea equipped with local bamboo teaspoons and a Noritake sugar bowl in tow. "Oh, I'd love to do that! You go first," she enthuses, setting down the tray.

In many ways, Corinne is the perfect blend of Yellowstone's Beth Dutton and TV Chef Rachel Ray… before that odd, slurring incident on social media.

As a civil service employee who's been stationed on the island for over five years, Corinne could well extend her stay indefinitely. We clicked almost immediately after I moved here. Corinne's warmth and outgoing nature contrast sharply with my own shyness, other than when I'm singing on stage, I'm not one for crowds, but she's taken me under her wing effortlessly. *She's trustworthy, isn't she?*

I take a deep breath and begin, "Okay, but all of this stays between us. Need-to-know only. Imagine locking this info away in a separate compartment, zipping your lip, and tossing away the key, my friend."

"Oh, don't worry about me. I'm the queen of compartmentalization," she assures with a playful cross of her heart and a zipping gesture over her lips.

Despite a lingering thread of doubt, I settle down in the living room and get Liam ready for bed. Praying he'll sleep despite the storm, I prepare for the possibility of a long night, thankful for the comfort of Corinne's recliner. He can just rest on me after he eats.

As I settle down to rock Liam to sleep, my brain feels numb, overloaded with the day's events. Needing some reassurance, I try to call my mom again, but all I get is a busy signal. Concern layers atop my existing stress.

"Corinne, do you know if there's some kind of power outage or something that might be affecting cell service? My mom had a long layover in Tokyo, and I can't seem to reach her cell. I just took her to the airport this afternoon to head back to the States."

"No, not that I'm aware of," Corinne replies thoughtfully. "But you know what? I'll ask at the Wing Commander's house," she adds, her tone light, knowing her current position gives her access to inside information.

"Thanks. Just keep it on the down-low, okay? I don't want to overreact," I say, trying to maintain a semblance of calm.

After a brief pause, curiosity gets the better of me. "So, how long do you think you'll stay on the island?"

Corinne seems momentarily taken aback by the question. "Oh, this is one of my favorite assignments as a civil servant, and I don't plan on leaving anytime soon. It's a great deal, really. And I'm making almost 50% more than I could back in the States because of the overseas pay. You know, the only person on base who's been here longer is our dear Della."

"Our local Godmother at Command Central? Did I ever tell you that's my maternal grandmother's name?" I muse, a small smile breaking through.

"Yes, she used to be a Department of Defense teacher here on base. After her husband of 40 years passed, she transitioned to a civil servant role at Command Central and just stayed. She's so kind, I swear, I want to be her when I finally decide to grow up!" Corinne chuckles.

"That's really something," I respond, pondering the quiet sacrifices of these dedicated individuals. "Hey, save that extra pay so we can plan a girls' trip soon!"

"I'm all in on that idea!" Corinne beams.

"Thanks again for hosting all three of us here. What's in this tea, by the way? It's like magic," I comment, feeling a wave of warmth and relaxation from the brew.

"Oh, it's my special blend. Do you like it? It should help you sleep, and you'll be able to get some good rest with Liam right here. Just tell me what you need, girl, because I am here for you," Corinne reassures me with a gentle smile.

"Thanks again," I mumble, my words slurring slightly as I recline back and settle Liam on my chest. "I'm so glad you civilians get to co-mingle with all the military families on this little island."

Corinne whispers softly, "I'm going to work on my menu. I'll be in the next room if you need anything."

Gratefully, I surrender to sleep.

Crack!

A sudden clap of thunder violently shakes the windows, jerking me from my slumber.

I bolt upright, disoriented. *What's that noise? Scratching at the window? Where am I?* Panic grips me as I realize I have no idea. Then I feel Liam's weight against my chest, his steady breathing reassuring me. *Okay, Liam is here with me.* My heart races as I try to piece together my surroundings.

And then it hits me... I'm at Corinne's, and we're safe.

My sudden movement and the loud thunder wake Liam, whose cries begin to cut through the lingering fog in my mind. Dazed but instinctive, I rise from the chair and start the familiar walk-and-bob routine to soothe him. Naki, picking up on the tension, starts to whine, but I gently shush her, guiding her back to sleep with a soft pat.

Eventually, Liam's cries subside, and his body relaxes against mine. We return to the chair, and I pull him close to my chest, trying to reclaim the calm. I think I hear Corinne moving around at the other end of the house, her presence a subtle comfort. Unsure but too exhausted to investigate, I let the rhythm of the rain lull us back into a restless sleep.

Saturday, 0600 hours (6am)
Corinne's House
Undisclosed Military Base, Okinawa

I startle awake to an eerie calm outside... the eye of the typhoon. Naki, picking up on the strange quiet, begins to whine. "Okay. Okay, baby girl, let's go outside," I murmur, shuffling towards the side chair to grab the oversized sweatpants I'd laid out the night before. Juggling Liam against my chest, I hop around on one leg, trying to slip into them. After a brief struggle, I manage to pull them up, whispering to Naki, "Come on, come on, come on," as we step outside.

The yard is still, the usual howling winds momentarily paused, as Naki dashes around, releasing her pent-up energy. The house behind us feels unusually quiet, and not just from the transient peace of the typhoon's eye.

Once Naki finishes her business, we head back inside. Just inches from my chair, I freeze. A peculiar tickling sensation crawls up my right leg, sending a chill down my spine. *What on earth is that?*

Panicking slightly, I reach down and slide my hand into my pant leg, fingers closing around a tiny intruder. Pulling out a squirming gecko by the tail, I let out a startled yelp and instinctively fling it across the room. The gecko scurries away, scrambling for cover.

In an instant, I'm doing what can only be described as the Jim Carrey 'Pet Detective' dance, shaking off the creepy-crawly feeling. The absurdity of the moment overtakes me, and despite the situation, I can't help but laugh at myself.

Catching my breath, I glance around to ensure no other surprise guests are lurking in my clothes. "Well, that was an adventure," I chuckle to myself, hoping the little gecko finds a less alarming place to explore. Glancing out the window, I note the stillness, enjoying the calm but wary of the storm's return.

I've survived baby poop, baby reflux, and all sorts of grossness, but a gecko in my pants during the eye of a typhoon? That almost does me in! In Okinawa, it's standard practice to shake out your clothes before dressing because local geckos love to sneak into cozy spots. Me? That wasn't even on my radar, not with the brief pause the typhoon gave us to take Naki outside.

Now Liam? He's definitely not a fan of my impromptu dance routine. His wailing is loud enough to raise the dead. After a moment to laugh at myself, I start the walk-and-bob to calm him down, my feet automatically carrying me to the kitchen where the smell of coffee brewing fills the air.

Corinne, ever the prepared personal chef, had set the local organic coffee to auto-brew on her sleek black Keurig. As I turn from the machine, my eyes catch sight of leftover crepes and an array of delicious treats on the counter. Starving and still buzzing from my gecko encounter, I scarf down a crepe, then another, savoring the rare treat I seldom get at home.

While I'm on my third crepe, Corinne walks in, shaking her umbrella dry and leaving it in the holder. I give her 'the look', surprised to find out she wasn't home earlier.

Corinne rolls her eyes, explaining quickly, "Wing command never takes a day off, even during a typhoon. I was just down the street prepping meals so they'd have something ready to heat up while we're all locked down. You wouldn't believe the menu changes I have to make once this storm passes. Oh, these are the days I question my sanity," she mutters, grabbing her own cup of coffee.

"Well, your magic tea worked wonders. Are we still up for recapping all the chaos to see if we can make some sense of it?" I ask, eager to unravel the day's events.

"Absolutely. Let's get comfortable here," she suggests, leading me to the living room.

We load up our laps with every blanket we can find. *When was the last time I allowed myself to just sit and cozy up? I can trust her, right? She seems a bit distracted, but her presence is reassuring.*

"Okay, it all started when we took my mom to the airport yesterday afternoon. Then, some young guy knocks over Liam's stroller, followed by the Master Chief showing up unannounced at our house. An hour later, a rock shatters Liam's bedroom window, and then a big explosion rocks the neighborhood. So, we're a little shaken up and definitely sleep-deprived... and voilà, you feed and shelter us. Did I miss anything?"

"That is A LOT," Corinne sympathizes, patting my shoulder reassuringly. "Well... I have news," she adds, barely containing her excitement. "Barbie and Lacey didn't make it home last night!"

Lesson 3:
Kugi San

Kintsugi –
Finding Beauty In Brokenness

Mom, I STILL SEE you! Even when life keeps throwing curveballs, we can find beauty in our brokenness and spread-thin moments, much like Ashley and Corinne have shown us.

I understand how you might be feeling, exhausted, overwhelmed, and questioning your sanity.

But what if we just sit with these emotions for a moment? Write them down and clear our heads.

Here's one of my favorite quotes that inspires me every time I pick up my pen: **"There is no greater agony than bearing an untold story inside you."** - Maya Angelou

Consider the following options and write about them in **The Warrior Mom™ Journal**:

1. **Steep Yourself in a Hobby**: Whether it's diving into a good book, crafting something beautiful, or trying a new activity, hobbies can provide a much-needed emotional lift.

2. **Go Outside**: Sometimes, just a short walk in the fresh air can be both calming and energizing. Connect with nature and let it rejuvenate your spirit.

3. **Celebrate Quick Wins**: Acknowledge and celebrate your achievements, no matter how small. It could be a successful nap time for your baby or a few moments of tranquility for yourself.

Remember, even the smallest steps toward finding joy in the moment can lead to significant changes in our lives. Every bit of beauty we discover in our day strengthens us and those around us.

Together, we are stronger.

I am with you,

Bren

Chapter Four

Yakuza Kyokuryu-kai (Okinawa Syndicate)

SATURDAY, 0900 HOURS (9AM)

Motobu Peninsula, Okinawa

In the dim morning light, The General carefully positions a package at the left corner of his massive, hand-carved desk. With deliberate, almost ceremonial precision, he arranges a dozen severed left pinky fingers in a perfectly aligned row.

SPLASH!

Ice-cold water cascades over Barbie and Lacey, eliciting screams of shock and chills from the biting cold.

"AGAIN!" The General commands, his voice devoid of any warmth.

Shivering, drenched, and still slightly intoxicated, Barbie and Lacey cough and gasp for air, their breaths almost synchronized in their shock.

"AGAIN!" Without hesitation, his lieutenants obey, dousing the two women with another bucket of frigid water.

It is only then, amidst her shivering realization, that Barbie notices her hands and feet are bound to the chair.

"You can't do this to us. Do you know who we are? This is against the Geneva Convention or something!" she screams, her words slurred by the remnants of sake.

"Very good. I trust you ladies are awake enough now to answer a few of my questions," the General growls menacingly from behind his desk.

Lacey, sobbing uncontrollably, pleads, "Why are you doing this to us? We didn't do anything. Why?!"

"You didn't do anything?" the General sneers, his disdain palpable. "Arrogant Americans!"

With a fierce slam of his fist on the desk, he startles them further, causing them to flinch violently.

"You ran over my legacy, my only heir. My family is the Yakuza Kyokuryu-kai now. You both will pay."

The air in the room thickens with the threat of retribution, the severity of the situation dawning on Barbie and Lacey as they realize the gravity of their predicament under the cold, calculating gaze of the Yakuza General.

0930 hours (9:30am)

Corinne's House

Undisclosed Military Base, Okinawa

Stunned by Corinne's revelation, I'm barely able to process her words when my phone interrupts us. "No freaking way! Hold that thought. This is Barbie's husband," I announce, urgency creeping into my voice as I answer the call.

"Mrs. Ransom, this is Commander Heisler. I'm checking back to see how you're holding up in this storm and if you've thought of anything new regarding the note you received last night," the Commander's voice comes through, professional yet tinged with concern.

"Oh, Commander, I'm actually shocked about the news with your wife and Lacey. Any word on them yet?" I inquire, shifting the topic to his personal crisis momentarily.

"Thank you, ma'am. A skilled team is currently searching for them. However, I'm actually calling about another matter. We've discovered some evidence on the rock used in the incident at your house. It appears someone sliced their hand while tearing the note and left behind a trace of blood along with some DNA. We're analyzing it now," he explains methodically.

"Interesting. Is this a type of injury that anyone might easily notice?" I ask, trying to piece together the clues.

"No, it's just a small paper cut. Most likely on their finger. Just to confirm, you, Liam, and Naki are all safe, correct?" he asks, reverting back to protocol.

"Yes, we're all safe. Corinne is sheltering us and feeding us well. When do you think we can get back into our own home?" I respond, my mind already racing ahead to when we might return to normalcy.

"It will likely be a few more days. With this storm, almost everyone is in lockdown for safety reasons," he replies, his tone implying the gravity of the situation.

"Oh! Did they give you any information about the explosion?" I ask, remembering the other unresolved chaos from the previous night.

"That's still under investigation. We'll update you as soon as we have more details," Commander Heisler assures me before wrapping up the call.

Hanging up, I turn back to Corinne, my thoughts swirling with the news of the DNA evidence and the ongoing search for Barbie and Lacey. "Where were we?" I ask, trying to regain focus on our previous conversation, the storm outside mirroring the turmoil unfolding around us.

0945 hours (9:45am)
Motobu Peninsula, Okinawa

Lacey's accusation rings sharply in the charged atmosphere of the room. "I didn't. She did!" she declares, jerking her head towards Barbie. Her eyes then catch sight of the gruesome display on the desk... dozens of severed pinky fingers lined up in a chilling order. "Hey! What is that awful mess on your desk? I think I'm gonna puke." And true to her words, Lacey promptly vomits all over the General's expensive Gucci loafers.

Each of the General's lieutenants, missing the last third of his left pinky, silently files into the room, their presence a stark reminder of their brutal loyalty.

"AMERICANS!" the General spits out the word with disgust. "This is Yubitsume. It is a sign of loyalty to cut the last third of the left pinky! Something you could never understand," he screams, his face contorted in rage as his subordinates scramble to clean the mess. "I want answers, and I want them right now!"

Barbie, still deliriously affected by the sake, giggles uncontrollably, oblivious to the gravity of the situation. Spit bubbles form at her lips as she slurs, "Yakuza? Nice try, buddy. That's mainland Japan action, not here. Are you trying to pull one over on us?"

In a flash of fury, the General hurls his sake glass into the wall just above their heads. The glass shatters with a sharp, echoing SMASH!

A heavy silence descends upon the room. The tension is palpable, thickening the air as the lieutenants quietly slink back into the shadows, their loyalty a stark contrast to the defiance of the captive Americans.

With a menacing glare, the General storms out of the room, leaving Barbie and Lacey in a state of shocked fear, their previous bravado evaporating in the face of the General's wrath. The severity of their situation is now unmistakably clear, and the storm outside seems almost benign compared to the storm brewing within the walls of the Yakuza stronghold.

1000 Hours (10am)
Corinne's House
Undisclosed Military Base, Okinawa

Corinne carefully places her "Chefs Heat Up Faster!" mug on the side table next to the sofa, revealing a small bandage wrapped around her left index finger.

"What happened?" I inquire, trying to sound nonchalant, but my mind is racing. *Hadn't Commander Heisler mentioned something about a possible cut on the hand of the person who threw the rock?*

"Oh, it's nothing, really. I was slicing melon at the Wing Commander's house, totally absorbed in eavesdropping on the conversation about the wonder-twins going missing. I missed the melon and got my finger instead. Occupational hazard," she explains with a light laugh, dismissing the injury as minor. "Now, tell me what you know, girl!"

I take a sip of the perfectly brewed coffee, feeling the warmth spread through me as the rain continues to batter the window.

"Here's the rundown so far. Lacey and Jim had a big argument because he didn't pass his Physical Training test. You know, all that extra he's carrying around the middle. If he doesn't pass his next PT, he'll lose his command, and she can't let that happen," I relay, watching Corinne's reaction closely.

Corinne nods, her expression turning sardonic. "What on earth would she do if she couldn't navigate her husband's career?" she adds sarcastically, clearly amused by the absurdity of the situation.

"Exactly!" I agree, feeling a mix of amusement and concern. "And then, she took off with Barbie, and no one in the spouses' group has heard from them since yesterday afternoon."

The gravity of the situation begins to settle between us, the lightness of our earlier banter fading into a more somber tone. Corinne shifts slightly, her eyes thoughtful as she processes the information, her bandaged finger momentarily forgotten as we delve deeper into the unfolding mystery surrounding people we know.

Lesson 4: Kugi Shi

Kiri Neru -The Fog of Sleep

Accept the Fog as Temporary

Many of us, like Ashley, Barbie, and Lacey, wake up feeling disoriented, looking in the mirror and hardly recognizing who we've become. Asking ourselves, 'Who am I now? I used to be vibrant, smart, sexy, and fun-loving!'

Today? We find ourselves racing around, trying to do what's best for our children, often getting lost in the relentless busyness of it all.

Daily Focus:

- **Acknowledge that sleep deprivation is part of the new-mom journey**, but remember, it is temporary.

- **Remind yourself that your body and mind will adjust** over time. This is just a phase, and you are adapting every day.

- **Prioritize sleep**, whether in small doses or long stretches. Rest is restorative and essential.

- **Nourish your body first**, and then, of course, your child's.

You can care for others better when you are cared for.

For moms of angst-fueled teens: Remember, it's biological. En-suring they get the right nutrition is critical. And remember, this intense period is a season, not a life sentence. A recent peer-reviewed study shows that teenagers need between 8 to 10 hours of sleep per night. Best of luck with this one.

Q.T.I.P. - Quit Taking It Personally. The moods, the attitudes, the slammed doors... it's not about you. Teens are navigating their own complex changes. Even small adjustments can begin to lift the fog, bit by bit. You're navigating a challenging time, but remember, every small step is progress. Accept that right here, right now, we are human beings, not human doings.

Write it out in **The Warrior Mom™ Journal.**

Together, We Are Stronger.

I am with you,

Bren

Chapter Five

Heion Jishin – Quiet Confidence

1015 Hours (10:15AM)

Motobu Peninsula, Okinawa

Cherry Blossom gently strokes her husband's cheek, her touch light against the fresh ink of his Tebori General's tattoo. "My Love, these two are older and have already birthed children; I really have no use for them in the Naha Casinos at this time. Reign in your temper, and let us get them cleaned up, then send them back to base with a believable story," she suggests with a soothing tone.

"You are right. What would I ever do without you, beloved?" he whispers back, his voice low, his hand covering hers. "You and our love are worth the war we must wage to claim this island as our own." Standing, he crosses the room to change into clean clothes. "You will handle the staff and get these dreadful Americans ready, yes? I will summon my lieutenants to have their vehicle ready in one hour."

Cherry Blossom nods and glides from their room towards his office. As she barks orders to her own troops, she turns on every light in the General's office. She finds the American women still drenched, hungover, and reeking of soured sake.

"Ladies, today is your lucky day! Operation 'Turn Back Time!' begins now," she declares, clapping her hands in an odd rhythm. Instantly, a dozen staff members appear.

"Wash their hair, remove their clothes, and scrub them thoroughly. Leave no marks! Bring my entire closet from the fourth-floor guest room. I am certain we can find something to dress these cows in," she commands with a tone of disgust.

"Hey! You can't talk to us like that," Barbie protests, struggling against each attempt to make her look more presentable.

"You are very fortunate that you are used goods, pathetic American. Or I would add you to my stable of women at the casinos," Cherry Blossom retorts coldly.

Barbie flinches, the gravity of her situation finally hitting her.

"But I didn't do anythiiiinng," whines Lacey, one more time.

"SILENCE! I will not listen to your whining for another second. You are guilty simply by being American," Cherry Blossom snaps, her patience wearing thin.

As the staff hustles to transform the two women, Cherry Blossom steps back, her expression unreadable. Her calm demeanor belies the swift, efficient action she commands, ensuring that by the time they leave, no trace of their ordeal remains visible... only the memory of it etched deep in their minds.

1130 Hours (11:30am)
Gordie's Burgers - Naha, Okinawa

"I'm so glad Gordie's is cool with dogs and babies," I whisper to Corinne as we settle into a patio table perfect for people-watching.

"Even as a personal chef, I have to admit I'm impressed with this place," Corinne remarks, her eyes scanning the menu appreciatively.

I secure Naki's leash to my chair, set up her portable water bowl, and fill it from the bottle I always carry. Liam giggles and reaches for me. "Time to feed the munchkin. I love how it's so normal to nurse in public here... with a cover, of course," I add hastily.

"Do what you gotta do. It feels great to get outside and really assess the storm damage," Corinne agrees, her gaze wandering over the remnants of the recent weather havoc.

"I know, right? These lockdowns are no joke, but I understand the safety reasons behind them," I respond as we both relax into the bustling atmosphere.

Suddenly, our server approaches, a bit unexpectedly. *American? That's unusual here. And he's too heavy-set to be a local.* We quickly place our orders, and I turn my attention back to Liam, nursing him discreetly while scanning the crowd. *Could one of these employees or even a patron be behind the rock through Liam's window?* The thought sends a shiver down my spine. I shake off the suspicion and try to focus on the positive, rejoining the conversation Corinne is having with the next table over.

"That's the other squadron commander who lives near me. They said no one's heard from Barbie and Lacey yet!" Corinne informs me, her voice tinged with concern.

"Whoa... didn't see that coming. I just assumed they were sleeping off a wild night somewhere. Oh, that reminds me, I need to call my mom again. I hate this weird sense of doom I'm feeling," I murmur, pulling out my phone with a growing sense of urgency.

1145 Hours (11:45am)
Motobu Peninsula, Okinawa

The General and his lieutenants escort a freshly detailed car through the circular drive in front of his expansive compound. The vehicle gleams as if it has just left the showroom floor, causing Barbie's and Lacey's jaws to drop in astonishment as they carefully navigate the front stairs in their sky-high stilettos.

"My baby looks brand new!" Barbie squeals in delight.

"Of course, it does. Nothing less for Yakuza," The General retorts sharply. "And it has a price. You ran over my heir. This is how it will go. This is not a negotiation." Turning to his wife, he whispers admiringly, "You have outdone yourself, beloved. These two look more presentable than even I thought possible."

"After all this time, you dare doubt my skills?" Cherry Blossom teases back, adjusting the signature cherry blossom in her hair, a daily reminder of her lethal legacy.

Barbie and Lacey glance uneasily at the trunk, now filled with glittery packets labeled "**Successful Gourmet**."

"What is this? Do we have to buy all these?" Lacey whines, confusion written across her face.

"Silence, woman! Listen to my husband and do as he says," Cherry Blossom snaps, her voice cold and commanding.

"You both owe the Yakuza an unpayable debt. You are now our perfect pipeline to the troops on your military base. These packets will give them better health, boundless energy, and clarity unmatched by anything your medical teams could hope to offer," The General states firmly.

Catching each other's eye, Barbie and Lacey share a look that screams, "We just won the lottery," their initial dread shifting to giddy anticipation.

"Starting right now, you both will be well-respected expert marketing liaisons selected by executives of Successful Gourmet. During the typhoon, you were merely detained in Naha because your new shipment of Successful Gourmet protein powder was being held at customs. You do not need to pre-buy anything. We will keep you supplied. You will sell all 2,000 packets by this time next week, or else. Do you completely understand?" The General lays out their task with chilling clarity.

"YES!" Barbie and Lacey shout in unison, their voices echoing in the near-silent driveway.

"One of my men will check in with you no later than Friday. All sales must go through this online app," he continues, airdropping the app to both their phones perched in the front console. "No Yen. No Dollars. Digital currency is only on this app. If you steal from the Yakuza, I will personally torture and kill your children in front of you. Now go!"

Barbie and Lacey peel out so quickly, gravel showers across the lawn.

"Well done, my love. Now let's see if they have more brains than beauty. If not, I'm more than ready to dust off my precision skills for when you finish with their children," Cherry Blossom purrs, her tone laced with menace as she takes her husband's hand and leads him back into the safety of their compound.

1200 Hours (Noon)

Gordie's Burgers - Naha, Okinawa

"Any luck reaching your mom yet?" Corinne asks as we finish off the last bites of what might be the best island food ever.

"Yes, finally. She let her phone die and then got delayed in Tokyo. Can you believe that? Here I was, imagining all sorts of worst-case scenarios!" I exhale, relieved yet frustrated.

"Look on the bright side, at least she's safe, right? Quick question," Corinne interjects, her eyes flicking to the keychain dangling from my purse. "I just noticed your Torii Gate keychain. It matches that scar on your left hand. What's the story there?"

"Oh, it was my granddad's. He served here during Operation Iceberg in 1945. He'd always get this haunted look whenever we asked him about it. You probably know more about the battle's history than I do," I muse, my voice trailing off. Then, gesturing to the scar, I continue, "This scar is a reminder of the only time I took the keychain away from my downright evil older cousin, Griffith, when I was six. He tried to use it for target practice. He and some teenager chased me through the north Texas woods, and I fell into an abandoned well. He ended up in juvenile detention for that. Last I heard, he was in San Quinto for an attempted murder charge. Can't pick our family, right?" I shudder, the memory still vivid.

"Wow! I had no clue Texas was still the wild west," Corinne jokes.

"I cut my hand on the keychain when I fell. Funny thing, every time I feel excited, the scar starts to burn a little. So if you see me scratching it, it just means I'm on the edge of a breakthrough," I explain, offering her a small smile.

Corinne nods her head. She's totally seen me do that before. I then point to the key chain itself, "Here, look on the back. I'm told Nakama means friend or comrade in Japanese. Granddad just said it was an important gift from a friend. That's technically Naki's name," I explain while petting my affectionate labradoodle. "We just shortened it to Naki to make it easier for all of us.

"No way! Really? So you sort of grew up with all this military lingo, huh?"

"Yep! Granddad would test us grandkids, making it a fun game. He and my Grammie always said I'd marry a military man. I used to laugh and say 'only if God was mad at me'," I recall fondly. "He passed away about five years ago. This keychain is one of my favorite reminders of him. We also named Liam after him. Oh! I almost forgot, I have a few of his battlefield journals. We could look through them sometime. Might be fun."

"Give yourself some grace, girl. You've been a little busy... hello, brand new mom here!" Corinne gestures dramatically towards Liam, "And I'd love to look over those journals. Sounds like a great mystery to solve!"

After our meal, I gather Liam and head to the restroom, while Corinne takes Naki and says a quick goodbye to her neighbors and meets me back at the van. As I secure the car seat, my phone buzzes with a message from Commander Heisler's executive:

> **You are cleared to return to your home.**

Just then, I spot Barbie's shiny sports car speeding past us, the Wonder Twins visible inside. "No way, you've got to be kidding me!"

"Let's follow them!" We jump into the Scooby van and tail them back to base.

Barbie screeches into her driveway, where a dozen cars are already lined up. "What is going on here, and where have these two been all this time?" I mutter to Corinne.

"No clue, but let's crash this party and act like we were invited!"

***

The atmosphere is electric as Lacey commands the room from the front. "Soooooooo glad you ladies could make it on such short notice," she gushes, her voice dripping with saccharine sweetness. "Barbie, please introduce our long-awaited surprise!"

With a flair for the dramatic, Barbie steps forward, her energy levels almost palpable. "Ladies, whether you want to get swimsuit-ready, your man in Maverick-level, shirtless volleyball shape, or capture your pre-baby bod, we have your answer!" she exclaims, her excitement bordering on manic. "We bring you the answer to all your goals. Introducing SUCCESSFUL GOURMET!!" The room erupts in applause.

Murmurs ripple through the crowd as one of Barbie's devotees leans over to her friend, whispering, "They weren't missing, just stuck in Naha getting their new product out of customs when the storm hit. Isn't this amazing?"

"We are going to be beach-worthy, girl!" her friend replies enthusiastically.

I can barely suppress a groan. *Who else drank this ridiculous Kool-Aid?*

"Oh, hello, Ashley. Did we extend an invite to you two?" Lacey sneers as we approach the table laden with glittery packets. I choose to ignore her barb and start examining the packets, but the labels are all in Japanese. *What the heck?*

Before I can muster a response, my cell phone vibrates with an incoming text. I glance down, a smile spreading across my face as I read the message:

DEUCE: Hey, babe! Wheels up. Landing in a few hours! Can't wait to see you! <3

Eagerly, I type back, my thumbs trembling with excitement:

ME: I'll time Liam's nap, get fresh sheets, and be ready for you

Turning to Corinne, I declare, "Hate to leave the party early, but we gotta go!" I grab her arm, pulling her towards the door. The promise of Deuce's return lifts my spirits immeasurably, casting a glow over the drab surroundings. Finally! My hero is coming home.

As we rush out, the sounds of the party fade behind us, replaced by the anticipation of reunion, warmth, and the comfort of family soon to be whole again.

Lesson 5:
Kugi Go

Heion Jishin – Quiet Confidence

Confidence is Quiet. Insecurity is Loud.

Think about this: How often have we, as moms, found ourselves in a group where there's always at least one person who exudes a kind of false bravado? You know the type: arrogant, overly assertive, and generally obnoxious. This is often a mask for deep-seated insecurity.

Heion translates to a peaceful or calm mind. **Jishin** means self-confidence, or trusting in oneself.

Daily Focus:

- **Respond, Don't React:** Pause before you speak. A moment of reflection can shift you from reacting impulsively to responding with calm, clarity, and intention.

- **Set Healthy Boundaries:** Start small. Say no to one thing that drains you or carve out an hour a week for something that fills your cup. Boundaries aren't walls, they're bridges to better balance.

- **Trust Your Mom-Intuition:** You know more than you

think you do. That gut feeling? It's there for a reason. Trust it, whether it's about your child, your choices, or your next brave step.

- **Seek Seasoned Counsel:** Who do you know that's walked this road ahead of you? Reach out. A wise voice in your corner can offer guidance, perspective, and peace.

- **Celebrate Quick Wins:** Small victories are still victories. A successful nap, a peaceful conversation, a quiet cup of coffee, all of it counts. Stack those wins.

Quiet confidence blooms from recognizing that you're doing your best, learning as you go, and that your love for your children is more than enough. It's okay if that confidence is just a whisper right now. It will grow louder with time.

Grab **The Warrior Mom™ Journal** and let's jot down three quick wins from this week. Let these small successes remind you to stay focused on your own path.

Together, We Are Stronger.

I am with you,

Bren

Chapter Six

Nakama - Friend, Comrade

The Yakuza General, lost in the world of his grandfather's note-book, reflects deeply on his inherited burdens and the shadows of a wartime past that still loom over his family's legacy.

80 Years Ago - 1945
0545 hours (5:45am)
Day 58 Operation Iceberg
Shuri Line Naha, Okinawa
I did not have a choice in our family's legacy. The Admiral made the choice for me. I remember it so clearly when he said:

'Colonel Takara, you are to escape and share with the Japanese Imperial Command what has happened here today,' Admiral Kinsuya demanded.

'But sir! I wish an honorable death with you and the other leadership on the suicide cliffs. My family will have a legacy of shame otherwise! I pleaded.

'You have the honor of being our liaison after we are gone. Secure all our priceless antiquities and guard them with your very life. Takara, you do realize that's what your name means. Am I making myself clear?!'

'Yes, sir!!' is all I could say in response.

I jumped into the flooding tunnel, engulfed with the scent of death and decay. I had to follow orders or suffer the consequences. If you are my descendant, know I had no say in the matter. I am the only living testimony of what happened here. During that time, I frequently patted my pocket to make sure they were there. I was given the matching Torii Gate keychains to access the treasures when the time came. If any of my belongings make it into your hands, remember san de waru. Divide by three."

"What are you reading, my love?" Cherry Blossom purrs, interrupting his brooding silence. "You have the most painful look on your face. What is bothering you so much? We are dominating this island, and very soon it will all be ours."

"Yes, my beloved, you are right, I am only reminding myself of why we must dominate," the General responds, his voice laced with resolve. "I was reading my grandfather's journal from the battle that happened on this godforsaken island, back in the forties. What a devastating loss. I will avenge his name and that of our entire legacy if it's the last thing I ever do!"

"Anything interesting I should know about? Like, where all those gorgeous antiquities ended up?" Cherry Blossom asks, her curiosity piqued.

The General hesitates, then replies, "First, I must get that matching keychain in order to open the vault with the treasures and figure out why that silly little American woman has it."

Our first attempt to retrieve it failed. I should have gotten one of our own, instead of hiring one of those desperate new American recruits, to do the airport job. And then the storm messed up our chance to discreetly intimidate her into giving it to us, with that message on the rock. There may be another clue to see if there is a workaround or if we absolutely need the other keychain, here in these journals. As soon as I know something, you will as well. I promise. We will find the treasure to fund our mission here. Now leave me to finish reading."

Respecting his need for solitude, Cherry Blossom knows the only thing left to do is to quietly leave the room and let him work. The general's fierce determination mirrors her own, and together, they are poised to unravel the secrets of the past to secure their future.

80 Years Ago - 1945
0550 hours (5:50am)
Day 58 Operation Iceberg
Shuri Line Naha, Okinawa

Monsoon rains lashed down mercilessly, nearly drowning me in my foxhole. As Private First Class Liam Rockham, I tried to find some rest on the muddy ground of Okinawa while holding the Shuri Line. I nudged my 6'5" bunkmate, Corpsman John Koshner, affectionately known as "Big John" to those who knew him well, making space for myself.

Coughing from the damp, I whisper-yelled, "Look alive, men. The enemy will be here soon!" Complete with hand signals, I directed my squad to shake off the relentless rain and flank the west side of the Shuri Line. War really is hell. The stench of decay filled the air, clogging my nostrils as the nauseating smell threatened to overcome me at the break of dawn. We had lost so many good men here; how had I become the senior ranking guy at that moment?

My goal was simple: to lead by example, not barking orders like those damn desk jockeys that called themselves officers. I started up the hill when suddenly the ground beneath me gave way. I found myself swimming through a tunnel flooded with the bodies of the fallen. A hand yanked me from the right, and I stared into the wild eyes of an enemy combatant. He whispered in desperation, "Nakama! Nakama! San de waru! San de waru!" before shoving something into my left jacket pocket as he was swept away by the current.

That's when a monstrously strong hand gripped my collar, yanking me back onto the battlefield.

Big John whispered, "Thought we lost ya there. Glad I could reach you!" Together, we trudged through knee-high sewage and sludge while rain hammered our helmets, threatening to drown us.

KABOOM!

Two men on our left flank went down, hit by shrapnel. The rest of us took cover. We tossed a friendly-colored smoke bomb so our air support knew not to target us. Bright blue. The color I swear I'll despise for as long as I live. I looked back to signal to the squad, my biggest mistake ever. At that moment, one of the enemies shot me at close range, and I hit the ground hard. As I administered my own morphine syrette, Big John appeared out of the smoke, handed me a cigarette, and lifted me onto a stretcher.

The next thing I remember? Waking up on a C-54, the propellers roaring. I checked my left jacket pocket and realized I was still holding the cryptic gift from the tunnel man. A bright red Torii Gate keychain with the word "Nakama" and coordinates "78.651, 383.1585" on the back. It looked like some kind of code. Whatever it was, it must have carried some good luck because I should have been a goner. Now that I think about it, we'd heard rumors of hidden treasure at Shuri Castle. It's probably bombed to hell by now.

What was the name on his uniform? Something with a T... Tak... Takara!

PRESENT DAY
1400 hours (2pm)
Major & Ashley Ransom's Home
Undisclosed Military Base - Okinawa

"NO WAY!!" Corinne gasps, visibly shocked as I finish reading my granddad's wartime journal entry. "He was here on Okinawa and a war hero! All this reminds me, have you ever read the book *The Girl With The White Flag* by Tomiko Higa?"

I nod in response. "Of course! The Wing Commander's wife includes it in all our welcome packets. It's amazing that a six or seven-year-old little girl could be so brave!" I pause, feeling the weight of history in my hands. "To answer your other question, our whole family's heard stories about this island all my life. But actually reading something in my Granddad's own handwriting... it's different. It brings so much more meaning to this keychain. I knew it was sentimental, but I had no idea about the depth of its history. I'm shocked he left it to me."

As I prepare to put Liam down for his nap, the laundry washer/dryer combo unit beeps, signaling the end of a cycle. I can hardly contain my excitement, knowing Deuce will be home soon.

"Hey, what's scribbled in the top right margin?" Corinne asks, peering over.

I glance where she points and see, in my granddad's precise handwriting:

Always 3, baby girl. Always 3

"Whoa, I can almost hear his voice saying this. When I was little, my granddad used to play encryption code games with us grandkids. He'd give us an encrypted code to decipher to win a small prize. And like it says here in his journal, we typically were able to solve the code by dividing the numbers by three."

"That is so cool, you did the decoding with him!" Corinne exclaims, her enthusiasm undimmed. She continues without missing a beat, "I wonder what happened to the Takara guy who was floating through a tunnel of dead bodies. Yuck. I mean, he must be super tough to survive something like that, right? You know what? I think there's a local group that's tried forever to decipher codes similar to this one. Let me take a look online. Then we get to talk strategy for this high-end Founders Gala with the local wealthy ones. It's actually happening at Shuri Castle after hours tomorrow night!"

"Oooooh, sounds amazing! Count us both in. But right now, ya gotta go. My major will be here any minute, and we need to catch up... if you know what I mean," I wink and flash Corinne a mischievous smile.

"Alright! Alright! I can take a hint!" Corinne laughs quietly as she heads towards the door, waving goodbye. As the door closes behind her, the quiet of the house wraps around me, the anticipation of Deuce's return filling every corner.

80 Years Ago - 1945

1600 hours (4pm) - Day 83 Operation Iceberg/ Shuri Line, Okinawa

I, Colonel Takara, found myself washed out onto the sewage drain just south of Shuri Castle, drenched and reeking of death. In a rush, I discarded my military uniform, ensuring I retained my one remaining

Torii Gate keychain, and hastily donned civilian attire from a nearby deceased, bloated body. I draped my uniform over him and assumed his identity, an English Professor, hoping the authorities would mistake this man for me. I then cowered my posture, melded into the crowd, and made my way into Naha. There, I inadvertently collided with a young girl, around six years old, waving a white flag. Her innocent distraction allowed me to pass the American soldiers unnoticed, blending in as just another local, miserable and ready to surrender.

Tasked with securing all antiquities of our Japanese heritage, I was astounded to be the sole keeper of knowledge about where these treasures were hidden. As I walked, I carefully turned the Torii Gate keychain in my pocket, its cipher 78.651 383.1585 engraved upon it, and prayed to my ancestors for protection.

Please understand that this ruse of mine, posing as a respected English Professor complete with round wire glasses and a tailored suit, successfully deceived those around me for nearly a month. Whatever tales you may have heard about my actions, know that this account is the unvarnished truth. It is my solemn vow to vindicate the legacy of our family, even if it is the last act I am able to perform. I shared the second Torii Gate Keychain with an American in desperation, as well as for safekeeping. The name on his uniform was Rockham.

Always remember: san de waru!

PRESENT DAY

1600 hours (4pm) - Ashley and Major Ransom's Home
Undisclosed Military Base, Okinawa

The house is so quiet as Liam naps, except for the soft hum of the refrigerator and the subtle tick-tick-tick of the clock on the wall. I seize the moment for a quick shower and apply Deuce's favorite lavender lotion all over my rebounding post-baby body. Slipping into one of the silk robes Deuce gifted me recently, I pace nervously by the window, fingers drumming a rhythm on the encoded message the Chief dropped off last week.

Finally, Deuce's car pulls into our driveway. I set the encoded message on my nightstand and rush to the entryway. My heart pounds with longing, a mixture of excitement and nervous anticipation builds with every second. It almost feels like he's making me wait on purpose as he hauls his go-bag out of the back passenger seat.

The door opens, and there he stands, my smoking hot and forever fierce husband. The sight of him in his uniform, the duffel bag slung over his shoulder, sends a wave of relief and longing crashing over me. Without hesitation, he closes the distance between us, resting a muscled arm across the back of my shoulders. Realizing that just won't cut it, he drops his bag, wrapping me in a full bear hug the size of Texas, his familiar scent, soap and a hint of gun oil, fills my senses.

"You're home," I whisper against his chest, holding him tightly, as if I can make up for all the days apart in this single moment.

Deuce caresses my face gently, his thumb brushing over my lips as he studies me with those deep, dark eyes I miss when he's away. "I missed you, babe. So much."

I attempt a smile while happy tears threaten to spill from my eyes. "Me too."

He leans down, pressing a tender kiss to my forehead, then my ear, teasing me before claiming my lips in a slow, burning kiss that speaks all the words we've yet to say. My fingers curl into his shirt, feeling the heat radiate from him beneath the fabric, grounding me in the reality that he is truly here, with me. Right here. Right now.

We stand in the entryway, consumed with each other, the world outside forgotten. His hand finds mine, our fingers lace together as he leads me further inside. The soft breeze off the lanai creates an intimacy that wraps around us like a whispered promise, carrying the scent of salt and orchids. His fingers trace gentle patterns along my back, each touch igniting a fire that dances over my skin.

I turn and gently caress the lines of his face, memorizing him all over again. "You look tired."

Deuce smiles, a weary but content expression on his face. "I am. But being here with you makes everything worth it."

I lead him to the bedroom, where we sink down together, limbs tangling naturally. "Tell me everything," I murmur.

He presses a hungry kiss to my neck. "Tomorrow. Right now, you're all mine, babe. Your very own Eagle has landed."

Light filters through gauze drapes, as we melt into each other. Warmth, strength, and tenderness. Desire, love, and passion. *Please, Liam, keep sleeping*. "Deuce, you ruin me for any other man. And when you use your mission call sign? I'm powerless."

"Then my work here is finished," he teases and begins to stand up.

"No, don't stop!"

"Your wish is command, babe."

And together we surrender to the gravity that's always pulled us back to each other, the space between us disappearing as his arms trap me beneath his rock-hard chest. My heart pounds in sync with his, every kiss, every touch, a reminder that no time or distance could ever change who we are together.

After making love, we sit in the quiet glow of the late afternoon, wrapped in each other and the soft sheets, our breaths still mingling in the hush of the moment. The world outside feels distant, unreal, as we exist only in this moment, our hearts speaking in the silence.

"You're amazing, you know that, right?" he sighs contentedly.

"You're not so bad yourself," I tease. I take a long, deep breath, indulging in the blissfully peaceful moment, then remember the cipher that came for us. "Oh hey, any chance you're up for a decrypt-sesh? I know, I know that's what you do for work, but this one's got me baffled. Pretty pleeeeeease?"

"I just got here. Give me a few minutes, and I'll be up for you all over again," he waggles those gorgeous brows and gives me a wink that dissolves me into a puddle of want.

"Deployment! It gives you a one-track mind, mister," I reply playfully, elbowing him in the ribs as I lean over to the nightstand and grab the coded message. "Liam won't sleep much longer. Take a quick look at this. The Master Chief of all people dropped this off while you were gone."

Deuce rolls his eyes playfully, but his curiosity gets the better of him as he unfolds the message. He reads aloud, his voice filling the quiet room:

"In the place where lions refuse sleep,
a hidden path the duo seeks.
Find the gate where progress stands,
guarding secrets of monoreeru and man.
Find the flying fox's wings,
touch each tip concurrently.
Use the sacred keys aligned
in the walls of the ancient shrine.
San de waru!"

As he finishes, a stunned look of recognition overtakes his features. "Hmm...this is a good one. I'm in."

The intensity of his expression, mixed with the intrigue of the riddle, sparks a sense of adventure between us. At that moment, it hits me, home isn't just a place. For me, it's simply and only him. His presence, his love, his companionship, they ground me and transform any space into a sanctuary. The challenges we face, like decoding this mysterious message, only deepen the bond we share, reinforcing that our connection is the truest form of home I've ever known.

Lesson 6:
Kugi Roku

Nakama – Friend, Comrade, Partner

"WE DON'T TALK MUCH, but I believe we have a more complete communion with one another than even lovers have." - *All Quiet on the Western Front*

Admittedly, I'm not naturally a history buff. Yet, living and working, breathing, and connecting with others on the island of Okinawa has changed me forever. This is where my son was born. This is where I began to evolve into who I'm meant to be. Here, I didn't have relatives or childhood friends to lean on, just other wives and moms on this tiny little island in the Pacific.

In the quote above, the author refers to the profound bond formed in the trenches of war. Isn't motherhood marked by a similar bond? When you see a pregnant woman in her third trimester during the suffocating heat of summer, you instinctively offer her a bottle of water and ask when she's due. It's a sort of sisterhood, and ultimately, it is what we choose to make of it.

Daily Focus:

- **Connect**: Encourage another mom today. It could be a simple compliment, a helpful gesture, or just a listening ear.

- **Be the Friend You Need**: Start small. Reach out to someone who might be struggling or simply needs a chat.

- **Write the Vision**: The Old Testament advises, "Write down the vision clearly... so that even a runner can read it on the run." Let's jot down three things we envision for ourselves as mothers and friends.

Grab **The Warrior Mom™ Journal**, and let's document three quick wins from this week, as we focus on being a *Nakama* to one another.

Together We Are Stronger,

I am with you,

Bren

Chapter Seven

*Giman – Deception,
fake or counterfeit*

FRIDAY 0500 HOURS (5AM)

Undisclosed Military Base, Okinawa

The relentless Okinawa sun beats down on the training grounds of the military base. Recruits stand in formation, their sweat-drenched PT gear clinging uncomfortably to their backs. Commander Heisler paces before them, his voice cutting through the humid air. "If you think the enemy's going to go easy on you because you're out of shape, think again. This week's PT test is your last chance to prove you belong here."

At the end of the line, Commander Linus stands stiffly, trying to blend into the background. He knows Commander Heisler's words aren't aimed directly at him, but they might as well be. Jim had been struggling with an extra 15 pounds that refused to budge, despite his best efforts at running and dieting. Failing his PT test again would mean losing his command for good. But that was his old self. In just ten days, he'd shed the weight, thanks to those miraculous smoothies Lacey had been concocting.

That night, Jim lays in bed, restless, staring at the ceiling while Lacey sleeps soundly beside him. He mutters to himself, "You've got to do something." Reaching into his nightstand, he pulls out a small plastic baggie with a scratched-off label. He tiptoes to the kitchen and blends another smoothie for a pre-test energy boost.

Jim hesitates as he recalls rumors of side effects: nausea, jitters, even heart problems. But his desperation drowns out the warnings. He gulps down the concoction, glancing at the microwave clock, which shows he still has two hours before he needs to leave. He tries to calm his nerves with some water and lies back down, waiting for the surge of energy.

When his alarm sounds, Jim feels a jolt of adrenaline. His heart races, and his mind buzzes with an unnatural alertness. At the PT test, he pushes himself to the limit. He sprints the final lap of the two-mile run faster than he's ever done, outpacing everyone, even those who usually lap him. His sit-ups and push-ups are a blur of motion, driven by a frenzied energy. When the scores are posted, Jim passes with a substantial margin.

"Commander, you were a machine out there this morning," Commander Heisler remarks, clapping Jim on the back with a grin. Jim manages a strained smile, but inside, he feels far from victorious. His hands shake uncontrollably, and his chest tightens with each breath. That night, he lies awake, his heart thumping loudly, resonating like the ceremonial drums at a local festival.

As days turn into a week, the Successful Gourmet powder becomes Jim's indispensable crutch. He starts every training session with a shake, depending on this artificial boost to maintain his performance. But as his body builds tolerance, the initial dose no longer suffices. Jim begins to double, then triple the quantity. The weight continues to drop off, but his energy levels plummet. He feels drained, like a machine sputtering on its last reserves. Jim finds himself wondering, *How long can I keep this up?*

0530 hours (5:30am)
Outside Gate 2
Undisclosed Military Base - Okinawa

"Why do we have to be here so freakin' early?" Lacey whines, adjusting her hoodie to cover more of her face.

"Suck it up. We're rolling in money, girl! And we're just getting started," Barbie retorts, elbowing her and giving her a look that quiets any further complaints. Scanning the dark parking lot, Barbie spots their contact. "There he is. At least we don't have to deal with that creepy assassin lady, Cherry Blossom. Cheer up. Grab the duffle and let's go."

"Okay, I got it. Just having a moment. Better now. Let's do this!" Lacey rallies herself, and they exit Barbie's sleek sports car, walking across the lot with all their duffles in tow.

"Show me!" barks a short Yakuza muscle man, not bothering to hide his impatience.

They both open their duffles to reveal thousands of empty packets, evidence of their recent sales.

The muscle guy nods to someone in the black Mercedes, and the door swings open.

"Show me as well!" booms The General from the early dawn darkness.

"Whoa, didn't expect to see him here this early," Lacey whispers, a hint of fear in her voice.

"Silence, whiny one, and open those duffles now," The General commands as he strides around the front of the vehicle. His face betrays a rare hint of satisfaction as the bags are opened.

Barbie, regaining her usual confidence, asserts, "Seeing is believing. You actually doubted us? We moved over two thousand units this week."

"Of course you did. What are the reports from your buyers so far?" The General probes, his voice steady and imposing.

"Um," Lacey stammers, "mostly positive."

"What do you mean mostly?!" The General's voice rises, a growl lacing his words as he steps closer, invading her personal space.

"Well, sir," Barbie interjects, aiming to deflect some of The General's ire from Lacey, "a few people, both civilian and active duty, have reported some concerning side effects like racing heartbeats, blurred vision, pounding headaches... things like that. One guy even ended up in the base emergency room with heart problems!"

The General's laughter pierces the still dawn, eerie and echoing. "You Americans are so weak. Did you think this was candy? And you, Ms. Heisler, are you actually growing a conscience after all the commissions we paid you this week?" He signals to his muscle man, who retrieves two full bags of a new product from the trunk. "Trade with him and be gone. Now!"

The Wonder Twins exchange the empty packets for full ones and race back to their vehicle as if fleeing from a predator. They speed away in less than a minute, the weight of the new duffles slowing them only slightly.

"That was too close for comfort," Lacey exhales once they're safely speeding away.

"He's better than his assassin wife, who mentioned trafficking us," Barbie quips, trying to lighten the mood. "Just think, this will all be worth it, especially when we bank seven figures before anyone wises up to what's going on. We got this, bestie!" She high-fives Lacey, who forces a smile.

As they drive back to base, Lacey turns her head to stare out the window, her mind overrun with uncertainty, doubt, and guilt. The weight of their actions and the reality of their situation begin to truly sink in.

Saturday 0600 Hours (6am)
Major & Ashley Ransom's Home
Undisclosed Military Base - Okinawa

"You're up early, babe. Is everything alright?" Deuce asks, a tone of concern threading through his voice.

"Oh, you know. Duty calls," I reply sarcastically as Liam latches on for his early morning feed.

"You don't fool me, babe. You've been up for hours. What have you discovered about our mysterious puzzle? No way you haven't taken a crack at it yet," Deuce probes, knowing me too well.

"You know me too well. First, that opening line:

In the place where lions refuse sleep, A hidden path the duo will seek.

Obviously, we're not in the jungles of Africa, at least not yet. Quick! What's the first thing you think of when you hear the word lion?"

"Me being me, I'd start with synonyms like leo, wild cat, puma, or king," Deuce responds.

"You're on the right track. Now think of local synonyms," I urge him, nudging his thought process with my free hand so he continues.

"Well, a lion pair in Japanese is Komainu, the dog-lion figure pair that is outside most local temples and houses."

The realization dawns on Deuce. "The statues on our front porch, of course," he exclaims, smacking his forehead in a moment of clarity. "BINGO:

In the place where lions refuse sleep.

So whatever the message is, this opening line refers to a location where these lion-dog statues are always vigilant. They guard entrances to keep evil spirits away... maybe local protesters too."

Liam becomes fussy, and I lower my voice to a near whisper, "See, we really are a great team."

Deuce plants a kiss on my cheek, then on Liam's head, as he prepares to leave. "I couldn't agree more. In more ways than one," he says with a wink. "I'm wrapping up a few things at the office, then we'll continue our global treasure hunt puzzle-solving when I get back. Be careful with my two most valuable treasures," he motions between Liam and me. "And PLEASE wait for me before you go off on your own to confirm these clues."

"Always am. You too. Oh! Remember, we have that fancy Gala thing tonight. Want me to pick up your dress uniform at the base cleaners for you?"

"Babe, remember I'm the son of a former Vice President? Tonight's event calls for my custom tuxedo. Our goal is to blend in, not draw attention to our military presence here on the island."

"Good thing he's the former VP, and not former president, no way could you be Ghost Ops with all that extra Secret Service security around," I remind him.

"No truer words spoken. I love what I do. See ya this afternoon."

I watch him leave, a pang of longing in my heart. *It's only for a few hours*, I remind myself.

Deuce's encrypted Ghost Phone buzzes with an incoming text:

> **Sit-Rep 1015 hours at my office. Be there.**

Deuce: Copy. Oscar-Mike.

Looks like I'm on the move to Colonel Moore's office.

Saturday 0930 (9:30am)

Motobu Peninsula, Okinawa

In the dim light of ceremonial lanterns, haunting shadows dance across the walls of the General's study. Cherry Blossom, embodying the quiet strength of a trained Yakuza assassin, remains motionless around the corner, observing her husband.

Suddenly, the General's fury breaks the silence as another sake glass shatters against the wall. "I WILL AVENGE MY FAMILY'S LEGACY IF IT'S THE LAST THING I EVER DO!" he roars into the emptiness.

"I may have a solution, my love, if you are open to hearing it," Cherry Blossom offers calmly from her position in the doorway.

"I am. You may enter and proceed," the General responds, his voice still echoing with traces of anger.

Stepping into the light, Cherry Blossom announces, "I secured two invites to tonight's Founders Gala at Shuri Castle. Our son will be under close watch by the staff, as if their lives depend on it, which, of course, they do. Meanwhile, we can attend the event and pursue the cryptic message from your grandfather," she explains, her voice measured and precise.

Pausing strategically, she adds, "Only if you are open to what I believe the message conveys. We will do as you wish," bowing deeply to emphasize her deference.

The General lets out a resigned sigh, heavy with frustration. "I am listening, my beloved."

"As soon as I learned of your challenge with his writings, I revisited all the encoded messages I received while operating within the Yakuza.

I believe the cipher is pointing us towards an ancient shrine," she reveals, her eyes searching his for any sign of doubt or disapproval.

"You have my attention. Get to the point," he commands, his impatience growing.

"Shuri, of course, dear," Cherry Blossom responds with a knowing smile.

"Your wisdom captivates me. I am, once again, listening. Please continue," the General invites, his tone softening.

"The next to last line of the message," she recites, *'in the walls of the ancient shrine.'*

"Shuri Castle is often referred to in ancient prose as 'the ancient shrine.' Are you willing to attend this event, even though it is unusual for us to do so? If yes, your custom tuxedo awaits in your ready room," she states, her voice low and confident.

Without another word, she glides out of his study, leaving the General to contemplate her proposal. As she departs, the General sits back in his chair, the weight of his family's legacy and the possibility of unlocking its secrets at Shuri Castle settling over him like the heavy Okinawan air.

Saturday 1000 hours (10am)
Major & Ashley Ransom's Home
Undisclosed Military Base, Okinawa

"Hello, Della. I was wondering if you could watch Liam tonight while we attend the Gala at Shuri?" I ask, balancing my active nearly five-month-old son on my left hip.

"Oh darlin', I'd love nothin' better but I'm attendin' that same event. I'll be representing Civil Servants here on the island, of course. Why don't ya try the Wing Commander's daughter? She's one of my former DOD students and just turned 18. She'd be a perfect fit. I'll see ya'll tonight, ya hear!" Della's voice is cheerful, yet apologetic.

"Thanks, I'll give her a call right now. See you tonight," I respond, hanging up just as Corinne opens my front door. "Hey, what's up?"

My phone beeps with a text. I pause to read it:

> **The plan is in motion. The players are in position. -Mamoru**

Corinne catches the puzzled look on my face as she sets down her award-winning pastries for us to sample. "As promised. There will be more goodies at the Gala tonight. Bad news?"

"Oh, this text must be spam. Any idea what 'Mamoru' means?" I ask, hoping for some insight.

"That's easy... *Mamoru* means keeper or guardian," Corinne says, rolling her eyes. "Always reminds me of *Guardians of the Galaxy*. The original, not that sorry excuse for a sequel."

"You are so handy to have around," I laugh. "And *thank you...* these look amazing. I'll see you tonight."

"Oh! Almost forgot," she chirps, spinning back toward me. "I volunteered you to sing both the Japanese and American national anthems at the Gala tonight. Figured it'd be perfect publicity for your holiday music launch."

"Great," I reply, not even pretending to be surprised. "Guess I'll go warm up these new-mom-tired vocal cords before we head out."

Corinne waves and heads back to her house next door. As she disappears behind her door, she pulls out her phone and hits redial.

Della answers instantly. "Yes."

"You might need to up your game. I don't think she's getting it," Corinne warns.

Della smiles, her voice calm and assured, "I will handle it. Failure is not an option."

The line goes dead.

Lesson 7: Kugi Sebun

Giman – Deception, fraud or counterfeit

"I'VE WRITTEN 11 BOOKS, but each time I think, 'uh oh, they're going to find out now. I've run a game on everybody, and they're going to find me out.'" Nobel Laureate, Maya Angelou

I don't know about you, but I've been there...right where Jim was. On the outside, things may look like success. But on the inside? You're quietly waiting for someone to call your bluff.

Imposter Syndrome is a psychological pattern where high-achieving individuals doubt their abilities and fear being exposed as a "fraud," despite clear evidence of their competence. It's especially common among mothers, who often feel the pressure to never drop the ball.

But here's the truth: You're not a fraud. You're just human. And you're doing better than you think.

Here are a few tips to combat Imposter Syndrome effectively:

Daily Focus:

1. **Notice Critical Voices:** Be aware when the voice in your

head is demeaning, critical, or discrediting. Decide whether to believe it or not.

2. **Growth vs. Fixed Mindset:** Adopt a Growth Mindset by asking, "What is this situation trying to teach me?" rather than succumbing to a Fixed Mindset that laments, "Why is this happening to me?"

3. **Journal Exercise:** Find the page in **The Warrior Mom™ Journal** with the "What If UP" and "What If DOWN" columns:

- **<u>What if Down Column:</u>** Ask yourself, "What if this doesn't work and they find out I'm a total fraud?" Write down every negative outcome you fear, aiming for at least five.

- **<u>What if Up Column:</u>** In contrast, ask, "What if this does work and they find out I'm a total success?" List all potential positive outcomes, aiming for a minimum of ten.

After completing this exercise, turn the page in your journal and write down three quick wins from this activity. Focus on nurturing your authentic self this week.

Together We Are Stronger.

I am with you,

Bren

Chapter Eight

Takara Hanto - Treasure Hunt

SATURDAY 1015 HOURS (10:15 AM)
Colonel Moore's Office
Undisclosed Military Base, Okinawa

Deuce tensely explains, "Sir, we have a situation. They know where I live."

Colonel Moore frowns deeply, skepticism lining his face. "What are you talking about, Major? Are you telling me the Yakuza faction on Oahu found out where you live over four thousand miles away? That's hard to believe, even for me," he grunts, leaning back in his chair.

"They sent a message through the Master Chief and left it with my wife when we were off-island. These people are ruthless, and I'm ready to bring them down!" Deuce's voice is firm, his resolve clear.

"Let's dial it back a notch, Major. We'll bring them down together. Once and for all," Colonel Moore asserts, his tone commanding yet reassuring.

"You're right. And it's going down tonight. The Founders Gala at Shuri Castle is the perfect setting. We can't sit on this," Deuce asserts, his strategy taking shape.

"Tell me what you know so I can make an informed decision. I'm listening," Moore prompts.

Deuce outlines the details of what he and Ashley had decoded from the mysterious message linked to the Yakuza.

"Skip the group transportation to the event. I'll arrange for one of our sergeants to transport you and your wife to the starting point before the Gala begins. Be ready no later than 1930 hours. Tell no one else what you know so far, especially that Chef, Corinne something. This is one loop she needs to be left out of right now. Copy?" Colonel Moore instructs, ensuring operational security.

"Understood," Deuce responds, his military training kicking in.

"And Major, locate that ceremonial tanto knife above all else. At sundown, use the cipher and head to Tamori Cemetery. My gut tells me this knife is another key to all your remaining clues."

"Copy, Sir."

Deuce walks out of the office, his mind racing with the weight of the mission. He heads back home, prepared for what might be one of the most crucial nights of his career.

Saturday 1045 Hours (10:45am)
Major & Ashley Ransom's Home
Undisclosed Military Base, Okinawa

"...Thanks, we need backup at 1955 hours. The team can't mess this up. Understood?" Deuce's tone leaves no room for doubt. It's more a command than a question.

"Copy that, Sir."

"Good." Deuce ends the call, slips his phone into his pocket, and brushes off his sleeves... a clear sign of his frustration with the current situation.

I walk into the room just as he finishes up. "Hey there, handsome. Who was that on your top-secret Bat Phone?"

"My team. And just a reminder, it's an encrypted Ghost Recon communications unit, babe."

"Copy that, Eagle-Rockstar-Commander-in-Chief," I mock salute and plop down in the chair next to our bed, playing along with his formal demeanor. "Hmmmmm...today seems to have all kinds of surprises. Della, you know, the southern grandmother Command Central Operator? She'll be at the Gala and can't watch Liam for us."

"Oh, I didn't realize civilians were invited. Who did you get to cover for us?"

"The Wing Commander's daughter. She's a legal adult now, just turned 18, and is CPR certified. It all seems to be working itself out. We have a few hours."

"I got it, babe. Any chance I'll get a private fashion show of you in that gorgeous evening gown before we head out?" Deuce's mood lightens, his eyes twinkling with a mix of anticipation and playfulness.

"If you're lucky," I wink and add a little extra wiggle to my runway strut as I walk down the hall to gather Liam and his items for the sitter tonight. As I pass the mirror, I practice the smile I'll need to keep my nerves under wraps for tonight's Gala.

Saturday 1330 Hours (1:30pm)
Motobu Peninsula, Okinawa

"General, we have incoming!" one of his lieutenants shouts, the urgency in his voice cutting through the serene afternoon like a siren. The sound of bullets tearing through the air soon follows, disrupting the calm of the General's compound.

"I will handle it. Get my wife and son to safety. Go. NOW!" the General commands, his voice a controlled explosion of authority and concern.

Moving with the precision of a seasoned warrior, he reaches for the lower right drawer of his hand-carved desk and quickly activates a hidden compartment. His hands are steady as he retrieves two fully loaded Mac-10 automatic weapons, his movements practiced and efficient.

With no time to spare, he rolls across the living room floor, taking a position that gives him a clear line of sight to the main entrance. The weapons in his hands come alive, spitting out a relentless stream of bullets at a rate of a thousand rounds per minute. His double-handed suppression fire creates a deadly barrier, providing the necessary cover for his family to make it to the safety of the secure room.

As bullets whiz by, his mind races with questions: *Who could possibly know where I live? Why launch such a brazen attack in broad daylight?* Fueled by adrenaline and a fierce protective instinct, he resolves that today's assailants will face their end. "Baka! These fools have chosen the wrong day to cross me," he mutters under his breath, tightening his grip on the weapons as he prepares to defend his home and family with lethal precision.

As the General provides cover, he watches through narrowed eyes as his lieutenants usher his wife and son into the fortified room, their figures blurring in his peripheral vision. The intensity of the gunfire doesn't let up; if anything, it intensifies as the attackers realize their easy target is far more formidable than anticipated.

As the last of his family disappears behind the reinforced door of the safe room, the General allows himself a brief moment to ensure their absolute safety before turning his full attention back to the fray. The sound of his guns fills the air, a deadly lullaby for the intruders who dared to disturb his dominion.

Saturday 1345 Hours (1:45pm)
A Hotel in Naha, Okinawa

A dark figure paces erratically in his small hotel room. The excitement and anticipation of being one step closer to his goal are making him almost manic with energy.

"Can't believe it's been two years since getting rid of Ashley's former fiancé. If only that Major hadn't gotten in the way! Could've had my hands on that Torii Gate keychain by now!"

He stops pacing and stares out the window, which offers a clear view of the East China Sea. The vast expanse of water reflects his turbulent thoughts.

"Tonight, nothing gets in the way. Not Ashley. Not the Major. Not even the Yakuza. That treasure is mine." His words echo slightly in the sparse room, blending with the sound of the waves crashing against the shore outside. The determination in his tone is palpable, a fierce resolve to claim what he believes is rightfully his.

Saturday 1400 Hours (2pm)
Major & Ashley Ransom's House
Undisclosed Military Base, Okinawa

"Babe, there's an issue near the north part of the island, we're spinning up. I'll wrap things up as soon as I can. Will you and Liam be OK for an hour or two?" Deuce asks, grabbing his go-bag.

"Of course, everything alright?" I respond, trying to mask the concern in my voice.

"Need to know and way above your pay grade," Deuce winks, injecting a bit of levity into the tension.

"Be careful with my favorite husband. Oh, and I already took Liam to the sitter's while you were in the shower," I say, handing him his jacket.

"I'm always careful. Ugh, we're alone, and I have to spin up?" He grumbles, half-joking, half-serious.

Deuce starts to open the front door, the instant his fingers curl around the doorknob and twist, our world explodes. A blast of heat slams into the room, knocking us further into the house. The door swings violently on its hinges, rattling like it's struck by a sledgehammer.

I choke on the acrid smoke filling our once quiet neighborhood. Through the widening gap, fire engulfs the street. A car, a dark sedan parked too close to the curb, is split apart by the explosion. Shards of metal, glass, and flame scatter like shrapnel, spinning through the smoke-filled air. A shockwave rattles the windows, sending a spider web of cracks across the window pane.

The roar of the blast drowns everything. The sound isn't just loud. It's a pressure, a force that swallows my breath, squeezes my lungs, and drowns my thoughts in raw, unfiltered panic.

As smoke pours from the wreckage, thick and stinging, curling in furious black tendrils against the pale afternoon sky. The car's skeleton is a charred, twisted ruin, as flames lick hungrily at what little remains.

Somewhere, pushing through the ringing in my ears, faint screams and frantic voices penetrate the chaos. Sirens? No, not yet. Just shock, terror, the stunned gasp of a neighborhood frozen in the grip of something too sudden, too violent to comprehend.

I push myself up, heart hammering, throat dry. A single thought claws its way through my stunned brain. Was anyone inside?

And then, a shadow emerges from the flames.

Saturday 1530 Hours (3:30pm)
Motobu Peninsula, Okinawa

As the General maneuvers through a lesser-known side door of his compound, the grim scene that greets him on his front lawn is a stark testament to the loyalty and efficiency of his men. Half a dozen Yakuza from the mainland lie bloodied and lifeless, their invasion attempt thwarted.

"We got you, boss. No one tries to take over this island without a fight," his most senior lieutenant reports with a stern voice filled with determination.

"Correct. Well done. Have the newer lieutenants begin digging a grave. One large grave out back. We will avenge this attack, after I confirm my wife and son are safe," the General commands, his voice steady as he marches back into his compound, his focus shifting toward the reinforced safe room.

He enters the safe room with an almost silent click of the sealed door releasing. Cherry Blossom and Kaz, shielded from the chaos, emerge from their temporary haven.

"Beautiful and artful battle by your lieutenants, love. I watched the entire thing on the security cameras while Kaz watched a cartoon, thankfully," Cherry Blossom says, her tone mixed with admiration and relief.

"Thank you for sparing him the violence. There is plenty of time to prepare him for his legacy," his tone softening slightly at the mention of his son.

"We must get ready and leave for the Gala. This feels like someone is trying to distract us, and we cannot lose sight of the bigger picture. We must focus on avenging your family. The treasure is ours!" The General nods curtly, his expression hardening as he agrees with Cherry Blossom's strategic insight.

Cherry Blossom nods in acknowledgment and adds, "I will meet you downstairs in one hour."

"Very well. Let us make it so," the General agrees, the weight of their shared mission clear in his resolve. Together, they prepare to confront the next phase of their plan, fortified by their recent victory and driven by a deep-seated need to reclaim what they believe is rightfully theirs.

Saturday 1600 Hours (4pm)
Major & Ashley Ransom's House
Undisclosed Military Base, Okinawa

The Base Fire Protection team rapidly extinguishes the roaring blaze outside our front door by 4 p.m.

"I thought I'd have a heart attack when the Captain came stomping out of that inferno," I whisper to Deuce, as we finish picking up debris from our front porch.

"Nah, you were nerves of steel. Just like your granddad taught you," he replies with a smile. "Let's leave the investigating to the experts while we clean up and get ready to go." I give him a look like he's nuts if he thinks we're still going.

"Babe, we're a Ghost Ops family. Of course, we're still going. It'll take more than an exploding car in front of our house to keep us from a black-tie Gala. Come on, let's talk inside," as he gently ushers me back into the house. Pulling out the Typhoon plywood from the entry closet, Deuce begins to cover our front door. "Listen, I know this seems scary, but we are so close to solving this encoded message. I believe that the car exploding was a clear message."

"Wait, what? You mean it was a 'Back Off or Die' kind of message?"

"I do. Someone doesn't want us to figure this out. So now... we finish it." I nod, comprehension slowly setting in. Deuce continues, "Now go on and get fancy, I got this. We'll pretend I'm prepping the house for another storm and carry on as usual. Fear is not an option. Our ride will be here in an hour."

"Ooooh, we might even have time for a little fashion show if I hurry!"

Saturday 1700 Hours (5pm)
Motobu Peninsula, Okinawa

Cherry Blossom lingers on the grand staircase as she enters the living room, the light catching the folds of her evening gown, making it shimmer with every step she descends. The General stops mid-conversation, captivated by her presence.

"My beloved, you belong in the movies wearing that stunning gown," his voice filled with admiration as he watches her approach.

"A wife is a shining reflection of her husband. I, for one, am thankful we chose our love over tradition," her arms wrapping around his neck, pulling him into a deep kiss.

"I am as well," he manages to say, his voice rough with emotion. "Let us go, before I take your specific sniper skills of steel and accuracy straight to our bedroom, beloved."

"You have the checkerboard cipher and the encoded message, yes?" she whispers into his ear, her breath warm against his skin.

"Of course, it is the only reason I am willing to attend this formal event. We will review it while our driver takes us into Naha. Come, let the games begin."

Together, they step out, the night air cool against their skin, ready to unravel the mysteries that await them at the Gala, with a plan set and hearts aligned.

Saturday 1715 Hours (5:15pm)
Major & Ashley Ransom's House
Undisclosed Military Base, Okinawa

"Oh my! My very own James Bond. Be still, my heart!" I fake a swoon and fall into Deuce's arms.

"The name is Ransom. Major Ransom, my pet," he says with his best British accent.

I roll my eyes, then cough to cover a laugh. Which he takes as a green light to deepen our embrace, kissing me senseless.

"Good thing I'm wearing smudge-proof lip stain, now isn't it, Deuce?" I joke.

"You always taste divine, babe. Do you have everything in that tiny handbag type thing you got there?"

"Oh, you noticed, did you? Check this out," I reply excitedly. When I open the mini-evening clutch, it unrolls to display all the tools a treasure-hunting Texas girl could ever need.

"What is all that?!"

"Well, from left to right we have my miniature lock picking set, a mini flash-bang, the cipher and coded message, a mini-pepper spray, and my most prized possession: my grandad's Torii Gate keychain," I giggle with excitement.

"I married a treasure hunter AND a warrior. How'd I get so lucky?"

"Now, let's revisit this message," I unfold it along with the cipher.

In the place where lions refuse sleep,

a hidden path the duo seeks.

Find the gate where progress stands,

guarding secrets of monoreeru and man.

Find the flying fox's wings,

touch each tip concurrently.

Use the sacred keys aligned,

in the walls of the ancient shrine.

San de waru!

Deuce purses his lips while looking at the message over my shoulder. "Monoreeru. Actually, the locals call it the 'Yui rail'."

"You mean the monorail?" I ask, intrigued.

"Yes, very good, babe."

"Hey, aren't there Komainu Dog statues at the Shuri station... the stop just a few minutes' walk to the actual Shuri Castle?"

"Correct, we'll make that our second stop. First, we need to head to Tamori Cemetery. You up for some sleuthing under the cover of darkness?"

"Always. Let me grab my clutch, and I'm ready."

Headlights flash through the kitchen window. "Hey Ash, our ride is here."

"One sec!" I rush back into the living room.

"Let's go out the undamaged door," he motions to the slider as we walk onto the lanai.

"Good evening, Major, Mrs. Ransom. Where do you want to start?"

"Tamori International Cemetery," I reply before Deuce even has a chance.

"What my beautiful bride said."

"Copy that."

I lean over to whisper in Deuce's ear, "Are you ready for this?"

"Babe, I was born ready. Let's go find the treasure."

Saturday 1800 Hours (6pm)
Transport from Motobu Peninsula, Okinawa

As the Mercedes S-Class sedan speeds through the darkening streets toward Shuri Station, the General and Cherry Blossom are enveloped in a cocoon of strategic plotting and intense anticipation.

"Good evening, General, where would you like for me to drive you first?" the senior lieutenant asks respectfully, bowing slightly as he glances in the rearview mirror.

"Straight to Shuri Station, near the castle, and make it quick," the General commands, his voice firm yet contained.

Cherry Blossom leans closer to her husband, her voice a playful whisper, "Dear, he is your most trusted lieutenant; he understands the stakes of our mission tonight."

"Let us not speak of failure, beloved. Our words have power, unimaginable power," the General replies, his gaze fixed on the dark road ahead as the city lights blur past.

The lieutenant nods, "Understood, sir," and accelerates, the powerful engine of the Mercedes humming smoothly.

As the General adjusts his seat, he activates a privacy partition between them and the driver. "We should focus on our strategy for tonight," he suggests, trying to steer their conversation away from distractions.

Cherry Blossom smiles, her hand sliding under the hem of her gown to reveal the thigh holster that cradles the ancient tanto dagger. "I have everything we need right here," she says, her voice a mix of mischief and seriousness as she presents the dagger.

"Why do you have my family's tanto dagger?" the General asks, his interest piqued by her unexpected preparation.

"I reexamined the cipher and the encoded message this afternoon. This dagger, along with your grandfather's keychain, are essential for unlocking the tunnel we believe leads to our treasure," Cherry Blossom explains, her fingers gently tracing the intricate handle of the tanto dagger.

Intrigued and now fully engaged in their tactical discussion, the General nods, "Then, it appears we are indeed prepared to claim what is rightfully ours."

Cherry Blossom leans in closer, her voice seductive yet sharp, "Together, we will dominate this island, not just by power, but by right and by strategy."

Saturday 1930 Hours (7:30pm)
Naha, Okinawa

The car ride to the Gala was filled with a rare, tranquil silence, a stark contrast to our usual bustling life. "Awwwh, our first night out on the town since Liam was born. Do you hear that?" I murmured, soaking in the calm.

"Hear what, babe?" Deuce's voice was a soft echo in the quiet of the car.

"Absolutely nothing!" I exclaimed softly, a small smile playing on my lips.

"Oh really, how about now?" In a playful shift, Deuce reached over to tickle me, his fingers dancing expertly in a way that left me gasping for air and clutching at my sides.

"STOP! Okay, I'll try to behave from this point," I managed between breaths, half-protesting, half-laughing. "I just recently birthed a whole human being here. This bladder isn't what it used to be, mister!"

He paused, his hands freezing mid-air as his eyes searched mine, a slight frown of concern replacing his mischievous grin. "Babe, I was playing around. Are you alright?"

"Of course, but I really don't want to ruin this evening gown, you beast. Now, act civilized and let's talk strategy. We're almost to Tamori," I chided lightly, smoothing the fabric of my gown as I compose myself.

Deuce straightens, adopting a more serious demeanor, which somehow makes him even more attractive. In his military commander-voice, a tone that both commands respect and hints at the depth of his experience, he begins, "Here's what we're going to do..."

As he outlines the plan, a sharp sudden tingling sensation spreads across the scar on my left hand. It wasn't just discomfort... it was as if the scar itself was reacting to the proximity of the Gala, or perhaps to the secrets we are about to uncover.

Lesson 8: Kugi Hachi

Shikata ga nai – Acceptance; Resilience

"A Warrior Mom knows that her scars only make her stronger." ~Bren Harris

Hello Warrior Mom! I see you. Isn't life just a grand treasure hunt sometimes? Today, let's talk about something every mom understands deeply: the scars we gather along the way.

Acceptance and **Resilience** aren't just words; they're lifelines. Here's a quick breakdown:

- **Acceptance**: Embracing reality with open arms, whether it's welcoming help, believing in our journey, or simply trusting the process.

- **Resilience**: This is all about being strong, flexible, and bouncing back no matter what life throws at us.

Motherhood can mark us with physical and emotional scars. For example, take my c-section scar, it's a daily reminder of acceptance and the beautiful reason behind it... the safe delivery of my amazing child.

And much like our main character, Ashley, we learn that our scars empower us, teaching us strength and resilience, when we let them.

Daily Focus:

1. **Reflect on the definitions above**: Consider the detailed definitions for **Acceptance** and **Resilience**. How do these concepts show up in your life?

2. **Journal**: In **The Warrior Mom™** Journal, dedicate a page to each concept. Write down how these ideas can be transformed into actionable attitudes.

3. **Personalize Your Path**: Identify specific actions you can take this week to embody these concepts. It could be as simple as accepting a compliment gracefully or tackling a challenge with newfound strength.

4. **Celebrate Your Wins**: At the end of the week, write down at least three "quick wins" you've achieved. Celebrating small victories is a vital part of building resilience and fostering acceptance. Write it out in **The Warrior Mom™ Journal.**

Warrior Mom, remember, our scars are stories of survival and badges of honor. They reflect not just where we've been, but also hint at where we are capable of going.

I am with you,

Bren

South Island 2

Tamori Cemetery

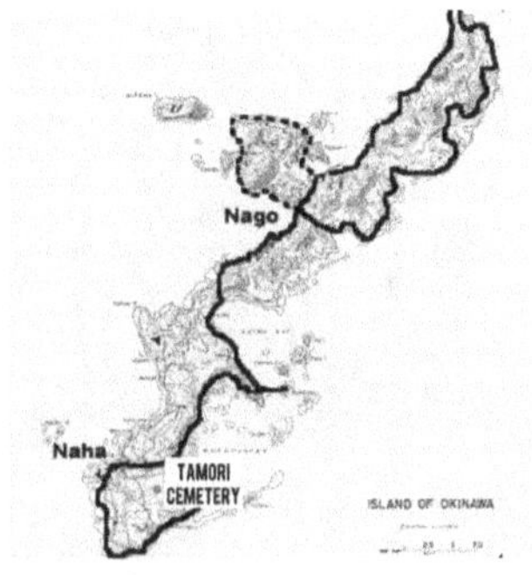

Chapter Nine

Tama Reien – Tamori Cemetery

SATURDAY 1915 HOURS (7:15PM)

Tamori Cemetery - Naha, Okinawa

"Sergeant, wait five minutes, then meet us here," Deuce tightly explains as he steps out of the squadron vehicle, leaving a small piece of paper on the front passenger seat.

"Understood. Call if you need backup before then, Sir."

The heavy full moon looms overhead, casting just enough light for the task at hand. I can only imagine the otsukimi, affectionately known as the local full moon viewing parties, celebrating this beautiful sight. Instead, here we are, about to trespass into Tamori Cemetery, one of the few Western-style graveyards on the island.

"Why do we have to sneak in?" I ask, though I already know the answer.

"It's closed after dark, by law," Deuce replies, guiding me through the Torii Gate and along the eastern path, careful to avoid walking directly over any graves.

"This is downright creepy," I whisper, clutching his hand tighter. His presence is the only thing keeping my nerves from fraying completely. "Are you sure we should be doing this?"

"Just trust me," he says, keeping his voice low. "Focus on the results. And remember, the coordinates only made sense after we divided by three. We're headed for row 15."

Counting under my breath, we turn at the fourteenth marker and follow his precise steps to the seventh headstone down the line. The tolling of nearby church bells sends a shiver down my spine, the sound mingling with the hoot of an owl and the flapping wings of a startled fruit bat.

"Almost there," Deuce reassures me, his grip tightening. He then removes his military-issue KA-BAR knife from its ankle holster, using the handle to tap a specific rhythm against the headstone. A secret compartment opens, revealing an ancient tanto knife we need for our next clue.

"Just close it, and let's get out of here!" I urge, as flashlight beams slice through the mist, converging on our position.

"Grave robbers?" I gasp, startled by the sudden appearance of several figures.

"Or worse," Deuce mutters, quickly wrapping the knife in a handkerchief and tucking it into his jacket. "Trust me?"

With a nod, I follow him as he leads us in a sprint across the cemetery, away from the advancing group. "Isn't that the way back?" I ask, breathless.

"Trust me, babe," he repeats, pulling me along until the Sergeant's vehicle screeches to a stop in front of us, the opposite direction from our original entry.

"Sir, get in! Let's go!" the Sergeant yells, as we dive into the backseat.

Deuce covers me with his body as the car pulls away, the sounds of our pursuers furiously pounding on the car's trunk. His presence, a mixture of warmth and reassurance, envelopes me in the cramped space of the backseat.

"Seems like you're quite the regular around these parts," I tease, trying to lighten the mood despite our rapid escape.

"Your Eagle has landed, babe," he smirks, the tension in his voice easing slightly. "Be careful, or the Sergeant might get more of a show than he signed up for."

"Can't help it. All this secret-agent stuff is kind of a turn-on," I admit with a playful wink, fanning myself for effect.

Deuce straightens, shifting back into his role as commander. "Sergeant, head to Shuri monorail station. And step on it!"

As the car speeds away from the cemetery, I lean back against Deuce, the thrill of the night's adventure pulsing through me like electricity. Whatever comes next, I know we're ready for it... together.

Saturday 1900 Hours (7pm)
En route to Shuri Monorail Station
Naha, Okinawa

The city glows in the fading light, neon signs flickering to life as the black Mercedes glides through the narrow streets of Naha. In the backseat, the General scowls at his phone.

"She is not showing up yet. The tracker we embedded in the child's car seat at the airport is not pinging. Signal must be blocked. But once she reaches the Gala, we will get a better lock on her phone."

He pauses, fingers tightening around the device. "It *is* her. Rockham's granddaughter. If it had not been in my grandfather's journal, I never would have known."

Cherry Blossom sits poised beside him, her evening gown flawless, her mind sharper still. "Brilliant planning, my love," she says calmly. "But why are we still crawling toward Shuri Station? We should have been there by now."

He presses a button, lowering the partition. "Lieutenant, our time of arrival is?"

"Seven minutes, sir," the driver responds crisply.

"Very well," the General says as the partition whirs back into place.

"You know," Cherry Blossom starts, her voice smooth as silk, "he has been with us long enough to lead his own Yakuza faction."

The General exhales deeply, his gaze still fixed on the phone screen. "I know, but his loyalty is too deep. He will not move without my blessing."

"Perhaps tonight, after we secure what we came for, you could offer it to him," she suggests, her voice a mixture of encouragement and command.

The General considers this, his expression unreadable. "Perhaps. Let us see how the evening unfolds."

The car continues its swift journey towards the monorail station, the city lights blurring past as they draw closer to their destination and the impending complexities of the night ahead.

Saturday 1930 Hours (7:30pm)
Shuri Monorail Station - Naha, Okinawa

"Come on, babe. We're running later than I expected. You know what to do, right?"

"Absolutely! Treasure Hunter and Warrior Mom, ready for action," I reply with a determined nod and a playful wink.

Deuce checks his watch, his expression serious. "On my mark... and GO!"

I dash to the station's entrance, quickly verifying the presence of the double Komainu Dogs that stand guard. Despite their formidable lore, they're smaller than I anticipated. I turn back to give Deuce the thumbs up, and he sprints off towards the ticket counter.

As I wait, a prickly sensation crawls up my spine, the distinct feeling of being watched. It's not the casual curiosity of locals intrigued by a foreigner in formal attire; this feels heavier, like the focused attention of someone with intent. I try to dismiss the discomfort, attributing it to the high stakes of our mission, and regroup with Deuce at the turnstile.

The moment we push through, the resonant beats of Eisa drums fill the air, vibrating intensely off the station's concrete walls. A troop of twenty drummers performs a robust routine, captivating the bustling crowd with their rhythmic mastery. The spectacle is both mesmerizing and overwhelming, setting a pulsating backdrop for our secretive endeavor.

Just as we're about to rush towards our next clue, my phone buzzes. I halt, heart skipping a beat. "Hold on, it might be the sitter," I say, extracting my phone from the clutch with slight trepidation. I unlock the screen to reveal the message, my fingers crossed for nothing amiss.

> *Find the flying fox's wings, touch each tip concurrently.*

Pressing into me and reading the text over my shoulder, Deuce whispers into my right ear, "Play it cool and let's focus on working the clue. We're obviously being watched. But together... We're better than anyone at this. What did you say about a flying fox earlier?"

I look around the station nervously, then remember whose granddaughter I am. "Um... yeah right, flying foxes... think... Fruit Bats!"

"What about them?"

"That's what the locals call them, because they're sneaky like foxes," I explain quickly.

Deuce furrows his brow and motions for me to continue.

"They eat all the fruit from the prized local gardens and ruin the harvest," I add.

"Right," Deuce nods, piecing things together. "So the message about following the flying fox's wings could mean something hidden or inconspicuous like those bats."

I spin slowly, absorbing the cryptic clue again: *Find the flying fox's wings, touch each tip concurrently.*

"One more time," I murmur, trying to quiet the growing impatience within me. We need to scour the area... ceilings, monorail cars, and wall art. Anywhere a fruit bat could lurk. "Let's split up and search. Quick!"

As I dart my eyes around the station, memories of granddad's training sessions flash through my mind, sharpening my focus. This isn't the time for hesitation.

"ASH! Over here!" Deuce's urgent whisper cuts through the cacophony of station noise, and he beckons me over excitedly.

There, concealed cleverly behind a group of vibrantly dancing drummers, is a striking mosaic depicting a fruit bat perched on a Banyan Tree branch, its wings outstretched and adorned with ripe figs, the very scene teeming with the clandestine allure of nature's thieves.

"We need a closer look at those wings," I suggest quietly, aware of the prying eyes that might be watching.

With a reassuring hand at the small of my back, Deuce navigates us closer to the art piece, maneuvering skillfully around the drummers.

Standing before the mosaic, I remind him of our plan. "We press both wing tips simultaneously. Ready for a bit of teamwork?"

"Babe, I was born ready for this," the corner of his mouth lifting in a half-smile.

"Typical," I roll my eyes playfully. "On three. 3... 2... 1 ...now!"

As our fingers make contact with the cool surface of the mosaic wings, a subtle but distinct click echoes slightly, hinting at mechanisms moving behind the wall.

Saturday 1910 Hours (7:10pm)
Shuri Monorail Station - Naha, Okinawa

"General, we have arrived at Shuri Station, sir," his lieutenant informs him.

"Thank you, Lieutenant. We will be staying at our Naha residence tonight. You may return to the compound on Motobu Peninsula."

"We are staying here tonight? When were you going to inform me, my love?"

"I thought I would add a bit of spontaneity to our evening. Are you pleasantly surprised?"

"I am, indeed. Wait! Is it not that the American woman who has the matching keychain to your grandfather's?" Cherry Blossom discreetly gestures towards the station entrance.

"It appears so. Quickly now!" They hasten their pace to the ticket booth. "I will secure our entrance. Keep your eyes on her."

"Already ahead of you." Cherry Blossom scans the bustling crowd as the General purchases their tickets. They quickly make their way through the turnstile, blending into the stream of commuters.

"She is accompanied, likely by her military husband. They headed in that direction." The General grasps her hand firmly, leading the chase.

"There, just past the drummers! The crowd around them is dancing... it is the perfect cover!" Cherry Blossom points out. Her voice is a mix of excitement and urgency as they navigate through the teeming multitude, their target just within sight.

Saturday 1915 Hours (7:15pm)
Shuri Monorail Station - Naha, Okinawa

As we attempt to focus over the soul-jarring rhythm of the Eisa drummers pounding their ancient rhythms, we press both wings on the bat mosaic. Their dance, a flurry of movement and color, provides the perfect cover for our actions. Suddenly, the wall behind the artwork creaks open. We quickly slip through the small entrance, and it snaps shut behind us, plunging us into pitch-black darkness.

"Oh my word, I swear on my grandmomma's prized sweet tea, what in the world just happened?" I gasp, the shock barely settling as Deuce brings up his phone's flashlight to pierce the darkness. "And this scar on my left hand is burning!"

"I, for one, am not the least bit surprised. You just cracked one of the toughest encryptions I've ever seen," Deuce praises, his voice echoing slightly in the confined space. Despite my formal attire and impractical heels, I clutch Deuce's hand tightly, determined not to let the eerie atmosphere deter us. Together, we venture deeper into the mythical underground tunnels beneath Shuri Castle, each step echoing into the unknown.

Saturday 1930 Hours (7:30pm)
Shuri Monorail Station - Naha, Okinawa

In the frenetic swirl of commuters and the thunderous cadence of Eisa drummers, the General and Cherry Blossom frantically search for any sign of the American couple. "WHERE DID THEY GO?!" the General bellows, barely audible over the relentless drumming.

Cherry Blossom takes a moment, centering herself amid the chaos. She scans the station meticulously like the trained assassin she is:

Drummers: 10 meters away

Commuter flow: 15 meters across

Turnstile: 20 meters to the left

Cross breeze: Negligible

Her eyes snap open, laser-focused. She murmurs to herself about the clue they had discussed: "Find the flying fox's wings, touch each tip concurrently."

Simultaneously, they spot the mosaic of a fruit bat with sprawling wings tucked behind the animated drummers. "Quickly! San-Ni-Ichi!" (3-2-1), she counts down, and they dart through the drummers to the artwork.

With adrenaline surging, a mysterious figure tails close behind the Yakuza couple, slipping through the opening just as the wall begins to close. The heavy stone grazes his shoulder, knocking him to the ground. "Made it! Not so high and mighty now, are you?" he mutters under his breath.

Communications crackle in the background from the Ghost Ops Team:

"Eagle checkpoint Alpha. Over."   "Samuri checkpoint Alpha. Over."

Inside the tunnel, I shout in disbelief, "Deuce! I knew it. The legend is real!" My voice echoes endlessly, revealing the vastness of the space. An automatic wall light flickers on as we enter the next section, casting eerie shadows along the ancient walls. "Guess we don't need my flashlight anymore," Deuce says, pocketing his phone.

"Ok, let's focus. We found the lions or Komainu Dogs, we nailed the flying foxes...what's next?" I ponder aloud as we approach a pictograph on the far tunnel wall.

"Well, what do we have here..." I muse, stepping closer to examine the image.

CLICK.

Deuce's voice cuts through the tension, sharp and urgent, "Babe!" I freeze mid-step. "You just stepped on a pressure plate. One move and this whole place goes up in flames." The weight of our predicament settles in as we stand motionless in the dimly lit tunnel, surrounded by history and peril.

Lesson 9:
Kugi Kyu

Shinrai – Trust; Confidence

"Trust is the oxygen of all human relationships, but it's also what trips you up after you've been burned." -Lisa Tyrkerst

Trust isn't just a nice-to-have; it's a must-have. Without it, navigating through the complexities of life, especially as mothers and leaders, becomes exponentially harder. Trust is what allows us to lean into relationships and challenges with open hearts and minds.

Here's what trust does:

- **Builds Belief:** It creates a foundation of belief in others and in the systems we engage with.

- **Fosters Confidence:** It gives us the confidence to be open and authentic, secure in the knowledge that our vulnerability is protected.

- **Ensures Safety:** It makes our relationships safe spaces where we can express our true selves without fear of judgment or harm.

When has trust deepened your relationships or eased your path? Conversely, consider the impact when trust was absent.

Daily Focus:

1. **Be Reliable and Consistent:** Like how Deuce and Ashley have each other's backs in the tunnel, each day let's embody reliability. In motherhood, consistency shows our children that they can rely on us, no matter what's going on in this world.

2. **Communicate Openly:** Owning up to our mistakes as soon as they happen teaches our children that it's okay to be imperfect and that honesty is valued over perfection.

3. **Show Empathy:** In an often harsh world, being a source of empathy and understanding for our children is crucial. It shows them that their feelings are valid and that they're not alone.

4. **Be Honest:** Honesty, especially about our limitations, builds trust. Letting our children know we don't have all the answers but are willing to find them together encourages a similar openness in them.

In The Warrior Mom™ Journal, choose one of the Daily Focus points to explore today. How can you integrate this aspect of trust into your daily interactions?

Let's commit to building trust every day, creating a safe, confident, and resilient community.

Together we are stronger.

I am with you,

Bren

Chapter Ten

Shuri Castle

Ghost Ops Team Communication:

"Eagle checkpoint Delta. Over."

"Samurai checkpoint Delta. Over."

Panic seizes me as reality sets in. "I did what now?" My voice is barely a whisper, overpowered by the echo of my heartbeat in the cavernous tunnel.

Deuce's response is calm, his voice a steady contrast to the rising fear in mine. "Stay very still, Ash. You're standin' on a pressure plate connected to an explosive."

I freeze, the words 'pressure plate' and 'explosive' igniting a storm of terror inside me. "I'm standing on a what now?!"

Deuce ignores my panic, focusing instead on the task at hand. He maneuvers a small boulder from the nearby rubble, weighing it in his hands, calculating. "This might not be heavy enough to trick the sensor when you move, but it's the best shot we have."

As a bead of sweat drips uncomfortably into my eye, my instinct is to wipe it away, but Deuce's sharp command stops me cold. "Do not move an inch," he orders, his teeth gritted in concentration.

"Right, just a habit," I reply, my voice shaky as I force my body into a statue-like stillness. "So much for a relaxing, child-free evening out, huh?"

He offers a tight smile, the kind that doesn't reach his eyes. "We'll have other nights. Right now, I need you to jump clear on my count. Are you ready?"

My heart thuds painfully against my ribcage. "Wait, on three or jump at three?"

"Follow my lead... on three. Ready? One, two, jump!"

Pressed against the cool, damp wall of the tunnel, Cherry Blossom's voice is a whisper laced with urgency, "What was that sound?!" Her eyes dart around, scanning the shadows for any sign of movement.

"It was a small explosive," the General murmurs back, his voice steady despite the tension. "Fortunately, they are still unaware we are tailing them. The element of surprise remains on our side, beloved."

He extends his hand, and Cherry Blossom takes it, her grip firm. Together, they navigate through the dimly lit passage, their steps silent against the stone floor.

As they move, Cherry Blossom scoffs softly, "They behave more like bumbling amateurs than treasure hunters."

The General nods, a smirk playing on his lips. "Indeed, they lack our finesse. Let us make sure their folly becomes our fortune."

Ghost Ops Communication:

"Eagle checkpoint Foxtrot. Over."

"Samurai checkpoint Foxtrot. Over."

Still trembling from the adrenaline rush, I hiss between clenched teeth, "Deuce! You counted '1-2-3 JUMP!' I wasn't ready for that!"

He looks at me, eyebrows raised, "Are you hurt? Seems like everything's intact to me," he replies, a hint of teasing in his tone.

"Stop joking around. We nearly got blown to pieces! Don't you ever get scared?"

With a calm smirk, Deuce replies, "Babe, I work in Ghost Ops... top-tier, high-stakes. Getting scared isn't part of the job description." He then shifts the topic, "By the way, I managed to capture a screenshot of that pictograph before the explosion. It might help us with the next clue: 'Use the sacred keys aligned.'"

He shows me his phone; the screen displays an intricate pictograph featuring a Torii Gate keychain and a ceremonial tanto knife, similar to the one we retrieved earlier at the cemetery. "Check this out! This imagery, it's so detailed," I marvel, noticing a mirror image on the opposite edge and some numbers at the base, most likely coordinates.

"That's right," Deuce nods. "Japanese traditions often involve duplicate safeguards regarding ancient treasures. It's about balance and ensuring only the worthy succeed."

I sigh, feeling the weight of our task. "But where on earth will we find another matching keychain and tanto knife at this stage of our search?" The frustration is palpable in my voice as the complexity of our quest deepens.

Ghost Ops Communication:

"Eagle checkpoint Gamma. Over."

"Samurai checkpoint Gamma. Over."

"Beloved, did you hear that? They do not even know another keychain exists. This is almost too good to be true."

"I should just take care of them from right here," Cherry Blossom hisses. "They are too ignorant to find such a treasure!"

The General responds with a calm tone, "Have you forgotten about the long-lost Imperial Japanese treasure that has eluded discovery since my grandfather's time? The legend's encoded message has kept it sealed for almost 80 years. Despite your prowess, we need those Americans with their keychain and tanto knife to access the sacred vault."

Cherry Blossom, slightly pacified but still tense, nods, "Very well, my love. We will let them lead us to our victory, then claim what is rightfully ours to dominate this island."

The General looks ahead, his voice firm, "Good. Now, let us continue. Our destiny awaits."

"Babe, I know you're frustrated, but remember, we uncover the path by solving each clue one at a time. What does this latest line suggest to you?" Deuce asks, redirecting the conversation.

I take a moment to collect my thoughts. "Well, the line 'Use the sacred keys aligned' implies we need to align both the keychain and the tanto knife at a specific place and time, just like my granddad taught me. The coordinates probably need to be divided by three, matching those on the back of my keychain."

Deuce looks ahead, his expression shifting to one of surprise. "Do you see that?"

Ahead, the path forks into two distinct tunnels. "Which way do we go?" I ask, feeling a rush of uncertainty.

"Let's think... there has to be a clue about which path to take. Let's check the message again and look for anything we might have missed that indicates the right path."

As the General and Cherry Blossom quietly follow, only catching snippets of the Americans' strategy, they make a calculated decision.

"Let them choose first, and we will take the opposite path," the General whispers, ensuring they maintain the element of surprise.

Cherry Blossom nods in agreement, her eyes scanning the shadows. "It is wiser to let them lead; they can clear any dangers ahead."

Suddenly, as they move stealthily, the General's foot catches on a loose stone. He stumbles slightly, his hand brushing against a cob-web-laced wall, disturbing a massive spider web. His other hand accidentally collides with a decrepit urn perched precariously on a nearby ledge. The urn teeters and falls, crashing to the ground with a dull thud that echoes ominously through the tunnel.

Cherry Blossom's eyes flash with irritation as she hisses under her breath, "Careful, my love. We must remain unseen and unheard. Our advantage lies in our silence."

The General, regaining his composure, nods grimly. "A minor misstep. Let us proceed with caution. The treasure and the power it represents are too important to risk with careless mistakes." They continue, more alert and wary of their surroundings, blending into the darkness of the tunnel as they follow the distant echoes of their unwitting guides.

A sudden noise in the distance momentarily distracts us. "What was that?" I ask, my nerves already on edge from the night's events.

Deuce shakes his head, trying to refocus my attention. "Don't worry about it. Could be anything down here. Let's not lose our heads over a noise. Now, look at the paths... close your eyes, then open them and trust your instincts."

With a deep breath, I close my eyes. The darkness behind my eyelids somehow feels comforting compared to the uncertainty of the tunnels. "Okay," I say, trying to steady my racing heart.

"Now open," Deuce instructs.

As my eyes snap open, the answer is instantly clear. The right tunnel, straight and promising, contrasts sharply with the left one, which curls away into darkness. "We're going right," I declare with more confidence than I actually feel.

Deuce grins, pleased with my decisiveness but still playful. "Lead on then... just remember the last time you led the way..."

Before I can respond, Deuce steps forward to take the lead, setting off a hidden tripwire. A barrage of poison darts flies terrifyingly close, zipping through the air where we stood moments before.

"Kuso! What was I thinking?!" Deuce curses under his breath, pulling me back against the tunnel wall. "That was too close. You okay?"

My heart pounds furiously, but I nod, grateful for his quick reaction. "Yeah, thanks to you. Let's be more careful. These tunnels are no joke."

With heightened caution, we proceed, mindful of the potential dangers that lurk in the shadows of Shuri Castle's ancient passageways.

The urgency in the General's voice cuts through the damp air as he and Cherry Blossom navigate the perilous left tunnel. With poison darts clattering ominously behind them, he grasps her hand tightly, pulling her forward with determination.

"Stay close and keep your head down!" he commands in a harsh whisper, leading them with swift precision through the serpentine path. Cherry Blossom, her senses heightened, follows closely, her training as an assassin keeping her movements graceful and silent despite the danger.

As they dodge another set of traps, Cherry Blossom can't help but admire the General's unwavering focus. "You truly believe this route will lead us to safety?" she asks, her voice a mix of skepticism and hope.

The General nods without slowing his pace. "It has to. The right choices in these tunnels are not about luck; they are about strategy and knowing Shuri's secrets as I do." His confidence reassures her, and together, they push forward, relying on each other's strengths to navigate the underground labyrinth.

Meanwhile, the sounds of the Americans grappling with their own challenges echo faintly off the stone walls, a stark reminder of the race against time and danger they all face in the pursuit of a hidden treasure.

In the shadows, a figure lurks just out of sight, his eyes locked on the retreating forms of the General and Cherry Blossom. He smirks to himself, contempt clear in his hushed mutterings. "She's overconfident, that one. Thinks she's got it all figured out," he scoffs, watching as the pair expertly navigates through the intricate and confusing tunnels of Shuri Castle.

Clutching a worn map and a flashlight that flickers intermittently, he stays a safe distance behind, careful not to alert them to his presence. "They know their way around. Smart money's on tailing them, let them clear the path, deal with whatever traps are up ahead," he reasons quietly, his voice barely a whisper.

His gaze shifts back to the path ahead, eyes narrowing as he anticipates the challenges to come. "If that major's wife slips up, well, that's one less competitor to worry about. Not my problem if she can't cut it."

His steps are calculated, each one taken with precision and care to avoid making noise, despite his ample size.

As the General and Cherry Blossom disappear around a bend, he quickens his pace slightly, eager not to lose sight of them. "Just gotta stay quiet, stay smart, and follow these two. They're my ticket to my treasure. I'm not about to let that slip away." His determination is palpable in the dimly lit tunnel, a stark contrast to the quiet cunning with which he moves.

Ghost Ops Communication:

"Eagle checkpoint Lima. Over."

"Samurai checkpoint Lima. Over."

"Are you hit?" Deuce inquires, concern etching his features.

"I'm okay, but my favorite evening bag isn't," I respond, lifting it to show him the dart embedded in its side, visible in the dim tunnel light.

As he helps me to my feet, Deuce apologizes, "Sorry about that. I'll be more careful. It seems this place has more defenses than we anticipated."

"It's fine, we knew this wouldn't be easy," I reassure him, turning on my flashlight to scan ahead. My beam catches something chilling... a finger bone, still attached to an arm. "Look at that!"

Deuce follows my light. "We're not the first ones here, obviously." He sets a careful pace. "Stay close and watch where you step. We'll make it through this together. We got this."

"My love, we will take a right in five steps... now, turn!" Cherry Blossom commands, her voice echoing slightly through the narrow corridor.

"You do realize I typically lead these expeditions, my beloved," the General comments with a hint of amusement in his tone.

"Yes, but as your personally trained assassin, I excel in navigating such confinements. Now, seven steps to the left... and turn!" Cherry Blossom counters smoothly, guiding them with precision.

Aww man, navigating through this darkness feels like stumbling around blindfolded. Thankfully, the sharp whispers of that assassin chick guide me well enough to keep me upright. She knows this place like the back of her hand. I bet that Major's wife would love to see me trip up, but that ain't happening. We're the ones closing in on my treasure, and we're gonna reach it first. And as for getting out of here? Well, not everyone's gonna make it back, that's for sure.

Ghost Ops Communication:
Eagle checkpoint November. Over."
Samurai checkpoint November. Over."

I notice a section of the wall that seems different, possibly retractable. On impulse, I rush past Deuce toward a modern keypad embedded in the wall, a stark contrast to the ancient stone surrounding it. Just as I extend my hand to enter the deciphered code, a gleaming tanto knife cuts through the thick, humid air. Reacting instinctively, I raise my left hand to deflect the blade, my evening bag intercepting the knife and taking another hit in this night's series of unexpected dangers.

Cherry Blossom's frustration boils over as she shouts, unable to hide her impatience any longer.

"ENOUGH!" The General counters sharply, his voice commanding and clear. "We need her keychain," he reminds her, bringing a sudden, tense silence over the group.

In this moment, the reality sets in for everyone involved: Cooperation is not just beneficial, it's necessary. They need to work together if they are to access the treasure.

Lurking in the shadows, the observer watches as the young woman briefly disappears from sight. The subtle sound of shuffling feet echoes through the tunnel... a clear sign that she's not far off. He smirks to himself, anticipation building. "She won't even see it coming," he mutters under his breath, ready to spring his trap.

Suddenly, a meaty hand grabs my shoulder as I try to cry out for Deuce's help. The stench of sweat and greed yanks my attention toward my attacker, who abruptly pulls me behind a cluster of jagged boulders. The sudden movement takes me by surprise, my heart racing as I stumble into the shadows.

The wall reluctantly begins to slide open, revealing only a few inches of space. In that instant, chaos erupts. Bullets whiz past as a sharp prick in my right rib cage signals a knife's intrusion. With a swift, adrenaline-fueled reaction, I twist out of my attacker's grasp and deliver a forceful shove with the heel of my hand right into his nose. Blood sprays wildly, painting the air and walls with a grim reminder of the danger we face.

"You stupid little brat!" the burly man snarls, blood gushing from his nose as he presses a meaty hand to his face. His voice is low and venomous, echoing through the narrow corridor like a curse. "Thought you'd outsmart me, didn't you? You're wrong. Give me that keychain! It was *mine*, not yours!"

He takes a staggering step forward, fury radiating from every pore. "You should've died in that abandoned well when you were a kid! And your sorry excuse for a fiancé? That sleazy lobbyist? He was supposed to get the keychain for me. But *he* failed."

A twisted smile curls his lips. "Well, I took care of *that*, didn't I?"

Exhausted by the desperate American man's rant, The General bellows "You will NOT get in our way!" With a surge of force, he tackles the bloodied man, sending a Torii Gate keychain skittering across the muddy tunnel floor.

Cherry Blossom steps out from the shadows, a 25m Japanese women's pistol gripped tightly in her left hand. Her breath heaves in heavy pants, fueled by fury. Her eyes, dark and relentless, mirror the pure hatred that has taken hold of her.

"FREEZE!" Deuce's command cuts through the chaos, his fingers tapping out a specific Morse code on his jawline. Instantly, Ghost Op forces converge on the scene, swiftly gaining control.

Deuce snatches the keychain from the muddy tunnel floor and deftly confiscates Cherry Blossom's tanto knife from my tattered evening bag.

Regaining my bearings, I rush to the newly revealed slots next to the sleek, modern keypad. Deuce and I each hold up our respective items, the keychains and the tanto knives. Exchanging determined nods, we insert each item into their precisely designed openings.

"Deuce, on three, ready?" I call out, positioning my fingers over the items.

"Babe, I was born..." he starts, his tone playful yet focused.

"THREE!" I interrupt, pressing the items into place without waiting.

With a rumble of ancient gears, the wall before us begins to slowly slide open, revealing the secrets it has guarded for decades.

We race through the entrance and are immediately brought to a standstill, both of us astounded and frozen in shock.

"Welcome, y'all!" Della greets us warmly, standing amidst a treasure trove of priceless Japanese antiquities.

"Della? What are you doing here?" I manage to ask, bewildered.

"Darlin', I'm not just here for the sunshine. My step-daddy's from Okinawa, and he asked me to help protect all these precious artifacts! Now, come take a closer look at these beauties."

We inch forward, our steps cautious, overwhelmed by the sight before us.

"Of all the treasure hunters who've tried to uncover this place, you two were the toughest to shake off. I was sure the graveyard team would've thrown you off our trail," Della chuckles.

As Ghost Ops rounds up the others, securing them efficiently, a familiar voice disrupts the moment.

"That treasure is all mine! Granddaddy promised it to me! You were supposed to be dead, brat!" the burly man yells at me.

"Griffith? Is that really you? What are you doing here?" I ask, shocked.

"You didn't even recognize me as your server at Gordie's, did you? Too self-absorbed, spilling family secrets to that chef lady."

"That was you? I had no idea. I thought you were still in San Quentin."

"That's what you get for thinking. Got out on good behavior," he sneers.

Deuce steps protectively in front of me. "Take them away, now!" he commands, and his team escorts Griffith, along with the General and Cherry Blossom, out of the chamber.

While they're led away, the General and Cherry Blossom exchange a look, "This is not the end!" he snarls directly at me.

Suddenly, cutting the tension, Corinne bursts into the chamber, her excitement palpable. "YEAH! I knew you'd crack it! You're the smartest friend I have!"

"You knew about this?" I ask.

"Not until recently. Once you started piecing together the message, Della brought me in to help. All this is as new to me as it is to you."

I embrace my friend tightly. "Thanks for having my back."

"Always," she replies.

"What now?" Deuce inquires, his gaze fixed on the vast array of treasures.

Della steps forward, her role as guardian clear. "As lead of The Treasure Keepers, I can offer you both a 1% finders fee, under the condition you sign a comprehensive nondisclosure agreement. No interviews, no press, absolutely no public disclosure of what's under Shuri Castle."

We exchange a look, silently agreeing. "And we're free to use the finder's fee as we see fit?" I confirm.

"Absolutely. We're not the reward police," Della replies with a wink.

"Then it's a deal," Deuce says, and we shake hands, still in awe of the ancient treasure glimmering all around us.

Corinne slips up beside me, gently takes my hand, and whispers, "Let's get you looking presentable. We don't need you singing both national anthems with tunnel mud on your face and a room full of VIPs watching."

I laugh. "What would I do without you?"

We giggle like schoolgirls as she leads me toward the grand staircase that winds up to the main ballroom of Shuri Castle.

Suddenly, Deuce pulls me into a strong embrace, planting a kiss so heartstopping it makes the whole tunnel shimmer. His cheek is smudged with a blend of Shuri tunnel mud and Okinawa's crystal coral sand. He grins, still holding me close.

"Knock 'em dead, babe," he whispers, brushing a strand of hair behind my ear. "You'll always be *my* treasure."

Lesson 10: Kugi Ju

Hoshu - Reward

"NOTHING IN LIFE IS impossible. The word itself says, 'I'm Possible!'" - Audrey Hepburn

Thank you, Warrior Mom, for sharing this journey with me. As we conclude with Deuce and Ashley finding the treasure and receiving their reward, let's reflect on a few concepts related to rewards:

- **Reward:** Something given in exchange for good behavior or work.

- **Prize:** A reward given as recognition of victory or success.

- **Award:** A mark of recognition given in honor of an achievement.

- **Trophy:** A physical representation of success or victory.

In motherhood, our daily efforts often go unnoticed. Yet, we understand the profound importance of acknowledging our own hard work. How often do we genuinely reward ourselves? If you're like many of us, it's probably not enough.

While there's no exhaustive study on the specific rewards of motherhood, here are a few points to consider that could enhance our daily life:

Daily Focus:

1. **Small, Frequent Rewards:** Implementing small, frequent rewards can be more beneficial than waiting for big ones that seldom come.

2. **Personalization is Key:** Tailor rewards to meet our personal desires or needs. This makes them more meaningful and satisfying.

3. **Mindfulness and Reflection:** These practices can significantly enhance our well-being. Take time to reflect on your achievements and the journey.

4. **Social Connections:** Maintaining strong social ties can be incredibly rewarding and supportive.

Choose one of the daily focus areas listed above. Write out a specific plan in **The Warrior Mom™** Journal to reward yourself every day this week. Recognize your efforts, and remember, you deserve acknowledgment and celebration.

Together We Are Stronger.

I am with you,

Bren

EPILOGUE

SUNDAY 1400 HOURS (2PM)
Major & Ashley Ransom's Home
Undisclosed Military Base - Okinawa

"News from the Island of Okinawa, in southern Japan!" announces the perky blonde anchor with characteristic flair. "Treasured antiquities, presumed lost during the World War II battle of Operation Iceberg, were recently uncovered and are set to be featured in the upcoming World Museum Exhibit!" I turn up the volume just enough to catch every detail. "Planning your next family vacation? Be sure to include this once-in-a-lifetime event in your itinerary, as the exhibit will tour museums worldwide over the next six months."

As the news fades into the background, I snuggle closer to Liam, enjoying the quiet afternoon with him and Deuce.

A gentle breeze wafts through the living room, rustling the curtains as Naki, content with her new toy, gnaws quietly nearby. Liam, nestled against my chest, chuckles softly in his sleep. Could life get any more perfect?

Suddenly, the Bat Phone rings, slicing through the serene moment.

Deuce snaps to attention and answers, "Major Ransom."

"Major, this is Colonel Moore. I have an update. Are you sitting down?"

"Yes, Sir," Deuce responds, his brow furrowed in concern.

"Commander Linus has stepped down from his command and provided a detailed sworn affidavit uncovering a drug ring operating right here on base."

"Whoa. Good thing I'm sitting down. Is anyone from Ghost Ops involved?"

"No, but it appears the Yakuza kingpin, known as 'The General' the one we apprehended last night, his group was the main supplier."

"Unbelievable. Who else is involved?"

"Two spouses from our own community: Commander Heisler's wife, Barbie, and Commander Linus's wife, Lacy."

Deuce mutters under his breath, "Whiskey Tango Foxtrot."

Rising carefully, still cradling Liam, I'm startled by Deuce's unusual outburst.

"It gets more complicated, Major. Please put me on speaker; this next part concerns both of you."

"Go ahead, Sir. My wife, Ashley, is with me now," Deuce says after he switches the phone to speaker mode.

"Mrs. Ransom, thank you for joining us. The woman our team captured last night in the tunnels? She's a trained Yakuza assassin."

My heart skips a beat as I exchange a worried glance with Deuce.

"And it gets worse," Colonel Moore continues. "At approximately 1330 hours (1:30pm) today, she feigned illness. When the guards unlocked her shackles to escort her to the restroom, she subdued them both and escaped. Unfortunately, the Yakuza General and your cousin also managed to flee."

I gasp, the room spinning slightly as the implications sink in.

"Currently, all three suspects are unaccounted for and at large on the island."

To Be Continued...

THANK YOU BEYOND WORDS to all who make my vision a reality through this book.

First, my inner circle at MP Virtual Solutions, SayThat Publishing, and of course, my favorite military consultant, John Harris.

Second, our amazing advance copy readers. Your time and talents make this an incredible tale of mystery, suspense, and romance: Miranda Anderson, Jennifer Bradley, Melissa Dyess, Brandy Grillo, Lisa Lively, Tenille Stewart, along with Howard & Janice Villiers.

To all the members of The Warrior Nation, this one is for you!

Write the vision. Make it plain, so a runner can read it on the run.

Index:

Kajinho - Pizza In The Sky Restaurant

Kariyushi Shirt - Japanese version of the Hawaiian Shirt

Lagrima Del Sol - Pineapple Wine made locally on Okinawa

Lanai - A porch or veranda

M-R

Mamoru - Guardian; keeper

Monoreeru - Monorail system on Okinawa

Motobu/ Motobu Peninsula - Located in the northern region of the island of Okinawa. Home to beautiful mansions and Pizza In The Sky

Naha Kuko - Naha Airport, Okinawa (Oka)

Naki/ Nakama - Comrade; friend

Need-To-Know - Mission-critical information only

Okasan - Mother

Oscar Mike - On my way

Otto Suru - Overwhelm

Over - End of a communication

Oyabun - Yakuza General or Senior Leader

Pizza In The Sky - Iconic Restaurant on Motobu Peninsula with the world's best pizza and even better views (**Kajinho**)

S-Z

Samurai - Japanese Warrior

Scooby Van - A Mid-1960's Chevrolet G-Body panel van or Dodge A100

Soba Soup - a Japanese noodle soup with thin buckwheat noodles ("soba) served in a flavorful broth typically made with dashi (a Japanese fish-based stock), soy sauce, and mirin

Successful Gourmet - A fictional direct sales company, set up by the Yakuza, to supply drug products to American Troops on the island

Sumi Ink - handcrafted plant-based tattoo ink used by traditional Tebori Tattoo practitioners

Sushi - Delicious rolls of rice with raw fish, vegetables, or egg

Tamori International Cemetery - One of only two Western-style above-ground cemeteries on the island of Okinawa. Located in the city of Naha

Tebori Tattoo - A traditional Japanese style of tattooing done by hand, usually with a handheld tool with needles attached to a bamboo rod

Treasure Keeper - Mamoru (guardian; keeper)

Whiskey Tango Foxtrot - WTF!

Yakuza - Japanese organized crime syndicate similar to the mafia, which traditionally values loyalty above all else

Yokohama - A seaport on Southeast Honshu in Central Mainland Japan

Yui Rail - Monorail system (above-ground subway) in Japan

MILITARY ALPHABET CODES

A: Alpha

B: Bravo

C: Charlie

D: Delta

E: Echo

F: Foxtrot

G: Golf

H: Hotel

I: India

J: Juliette

K: Kilo

L: Lima

M: Mike

N: November

O: Oscar

P: Papa

Q: Quebec

R: Romeo

S: Sierra

T: Tango

U: Uniform

V: Victor

W: Whiskey

X: X-ray

Y: Yankee

Z: Zulu

<u>MILITARY TIME CODES:</u>

0000: Zero Hundred Hours (Midnight)

0100: Zero One Hundred Hours (1 a.m.)

0200: Zero Two Hundred Hours (2 a.m.)

0300: Zero Three Hundred Hours (3 a.m.)

0400: Zero Four Hundred Hours (4 a.m.)

0500: Zero Five Hundred Hours (5 a.m.)

0600: Zero Six Hundred Hours (6 a.m.)

0700: Zero Seven Hundred Hours (7 a.m.)

0800: Zero Eight Hundred Hours (8 a.m.)

0900: Zero Nine Hundred Hours (9 a.m.)

1000: Zero Ten Hundred Hours (10 a.m.)

1100: Zero Eleven Hundred Hours (11 a.m.)

1200: Zero Twelve Hundred Hours (Noon)

1300: Zero Thirteen Hundred Hours (1 p.m.)

1400: Zero Fourteen Hundred Hours (2 p.m.)

1500: Zero Fifteen Hundred Hours (3 p.m.)

1600: Zero Sixteen Hundred Hours (4 p.m.)

1700: Zero Seventeen Hundred Hours (5 p.m.)

1800: Zero Eighteen Hundred Hours (6 p.m.)

1900: Zero Nineteen Hundred Hours (7 p.m.)

2000: Zero Twenty Hundred Hours (8 p.m.)

2100: Zero Twenty-One Hundred Hours (9 p.m.)

2200: Zero Twenty-Two Hundred Hours (10 p.m.)

2300: Zero Twenty-Three Hundred Hours (11 p.m.)

LESSONS:

Lesson 1: Kugi Ichi - Moai - I see you. You are safe here.

Lesson 2: Kugi Nu   - Atto Suru - Overwhelm

Lesson 3: Kugi San   - Kintsugi - Finding Beauty In Brokenness

Lesson 4: Kugi Shi - Kiri Neru -The Fog of Sleep

Lesson 5: Kugi Go - Heion Jishin - Quiet Confidence

Lesson 6: Kugi Roku - Nakama - Friend, Comrade, Partner

Lesson 7: Kugi Sebun - Giman - Deceit; Fraud

Lesson 8: Kugi Hachi- Shikata ga nai - Acceptance; Resilience

Lesson 9: Kugi Ku - Trust

Lesson 10: Kugi Ju - Reward

CHARACTERS:

<u>Top Tier Operators</u> -

Ashley Ransom (Babe)

Major Anthony 'Eagle' Ransom, II (Deuce)

Cherry 'Assassin' Blossom (Beloved)

General "Samurai" XYZ (My Love)

Corinne (chef)

Della (Command Central)

Griffith (Creepy older cousin)

<u>Second Tier Operators</u> -

Commander Heisler

Barbie Heisler

Commander 'Spineless' Linus

Lacy Linus

The Coven Chicks

Famous Tebori Master

Yakuza LT's

Mamoru - Treasure Keepers

Quick Wins For Special Needs Moms

AMERICAN SIGN LANGUAGE

www.youtube.com

Signing time with Alex and Leah full episodes

Caregiver Support Groups

No Longer Just Parenting

https://www.facebook.com/share/1AZ2w3WoA3/?mibextid=wwXIfr

Mother 2 Mother

https://www.facebook.com/share/17r5AG9kSz/?mibextid=wwXIfr

COPAA - Council of Parent Attorneys and Advocates

COPAA believes effective educational programs for children with disabilities can only be developed and implemented with collaboration between parents and educators as equal parties.

About COPAA - Council of Parent Attorneys and Advocates, Inc.
https://www.copaa.org/page/about

Individual Education Plan (IEP)

ALSO SEE: Parent Center Hub Resources link below to find your state's Parent Center. They will assist you with the entire IEP process.

An Individualized Education Program (IEP) is a written document outlining the educational plan for students with disabilities in the United States. It's a legally mandated document under the Individuals with Disabilities Education Act (IDEA) that guarantees a free and appropriate public education (FAPE) for eligible students. The IEP is developed collaboratively by a team of specialists, including parents, teachers, and administrators, to address the student's unique needs and support their academic progress.

Parent Center Hub Resources

Works with families of children with disabilities, birth to 26 years of age. Find your state's Parent Center here. As of this writing, there are 100 Parent Centers across the U.S.

https://www.parentcenterhub.org/find-your-center/

Respite Care: help or assistance with your child diagnosed with special needs.

Find a Respite Provider | ARCH National Respite Network & Resource Center

https://archrespite.org/caregiver-resources/respitelocator/

<u>VAERS</u> - Vaccine Adverse Event Reporting System (VAERS)

The Vaccine Adverse Event Reporting System (VAERS) is a national early warning system for monitoring the safety of vaccines after they are licensed and available for use. It's co-managed by the FDA and CDC and serves as a platform for anyone to report potential adverse events or side effects after vaccination. VAERS helps identify potential safety issues with vaccines and can prompt further investigation if necessary.

COMING SOON:

"The General & The Assassin. A Warrior Mom Mystery"

"The Chef & The C.I.A. A Warrior Mom Mystery"

About the Author

Bren Harris writes mystery, suspense, and romance, always with a dash of real-life wisdom for mom.

Inspired by her journey as a mom to a special needs teen, Bren weaves stories that celebrate quick wins, inner strength, and the everyday heroism of women who give their all. She believes every mom deserves to feel seen, heard, and deeply valued.

Bren lives in Oklahoma with her family and two spirited fur babies.

<u>Connect with Bren Harris</u> – The Warrior Mom™

www.thewarriornation.com

instagram.com/winwithbren/

www.ingramcontent.com/pod-product-compliance
Lightning Source LLC
Chambersburg PA
CBHW071417300726
48976CB00004B/1152